MOSCOW ROAD

ALSO BY SIMON HARVESTER

DRAGON ROAD

NAMELESS ROAD

TREACHEROUS ROAD

ZION ROAD

Simon Harvester

MOSCOW ROAD

Walker and Company
New York

First published in the United States of America in 1971 by the Walker Publishing Company, Inc.

ISBN: 0-8027-5223-3

Library of Congress Catalog Card Number: 78-142843

Printed in the United States of America from type set in the United Kingdom.

For

SAM

who gave help in Berlin

'We great Russians have always acted like boors towards subject peoples. All we do is suppress them.'

LENIN

'. . . every foreigner in the U.S.S.R. is a potential spy: more than one sharp eye must therefore be kept on him, and he must never be trusted.'

SVETLANA ALLILUYEVA:

Only One Year

1

Midnight was near, the midnight of a warm cloudless Saturday in early June. Since noon the threatened enclave of West Berlin had been preoccupied with pleasure, noisy and gregarious amid the concrete newness spreading from the brooding ruin of the Kaiser Wilhelm Memorial Church. Today as on every day of relaxation its embattled and industrious people extracted enjoyment from every hour in case a near tomorrow replaced their freedom with the chill dictatorship which shrouded Nazi-style East Berlin beyond the grey-green barbed-wire festooned vileness of *die Mauer,* the Wall.

Although people admitted privately that they often felt as if they camped on a tightrope without a net beneath them it did not undermine their courage.

Here no one feared the police. Student demonstrations proved that. Beyond the Wall everyone was frightened of the Vopos, the People's Police. In East Berlin fear ruled.

One particular quality linked contemporary West Berlin with the city's ancient role of a warrior camp. Unmistakably it was a masculine city. Its men displayed pride in manhood. Their attitude was actively encouraged by their womenfolk. On days such as this every woman seen along the Kurfurstendamm and around the Tiergarten, at the Opera and the Schiller Theatre and cinemas, at concerts and in parks, waiting for an airplane to touch down at Tempelhof, passed on a thousand pavements, had an atmosphere of satisfaction at being a woman in a man's town. This proved them to be shrewd psychologists. They realized that the positive masculinity of their men and growing sons was the surest method of keeping alive their communal defiance and personal contentment inside the camp which ended everywhere at the hostile Wall.

Since dusk a heady buoyancy had pervaded the June night. On such a night it was possible to forget the city was one step away from being a prison. People were relaxed. Hundreds of West Berliners were still out. They strolled along the main streets or sat at cafe tables or drove home at a leisurely pace after an entertainment or dinner out or a visit to friends, enjoying the warmth and peacefulness. A grey-haired couple stood hand-in-hand watching heat-drugged white moths tumble dizzily in the beam of a car headlight facing the Brandenburg Gate.

Every apartment block and hotel had broken rows of pale yellow or pink or ghostly white windows. One after another was being blotted into the darkness above the luminous city haze. A quantity were sprinkled along upper floors of recently built blocks of flats around Lützowstrasse and within a short distance of *die Mauer* and one of its *Todeslauf* strips, the mined death-run sections, and the Brandenburg Gate, the Tiergarten and the Europa Centre.

Some of those who had dined and wined well inclined to weave somewhat as they headed towards their destination for the night. Or part of it.

Among those who had difficulty in keeping their balance was Dorian Silk. His companion, her arm linked strongly through his, was distinctly unsteady. Since they bedded her car down in its stable and started to walk to the block off Lutzowstrasse where she lived, he had wished that one or other of them had an extra pair of legs. As they went through a long patch of shadow, occupied only by an old empty Simca parked alongside the kerb, she increased the navigational hazards considerably by leaning on him affectionately. Somehow they managed to reach the block and pass through its swing-doors without mishap. But she stumbled as they reached one of the lifts waiting behind its iron grille gates and he had to half-carry her into the cage.

Their ascent to the fourteenth floor was memorable. She held onto him after it ended. Her mouth paid his the compliment of implying he had just invented a spell-binding new purpose for it, unknown to anyone since the original Adam wondered if women could do anything except hard manual work while he got on with his thinking. At this first sample he could understand why such a mouth was classified as an occupational hazard and strong men demanded danger money to stiffen their morale.

She let the occupation dwell on their senses for a while. Then she let him share the intimacy of the shiver which went through her. Being a simple man he did not believe any of it. But it was pleasant. As if unable to endure such maddening delight she retreated a full sixteenth of an inch.

'Ah Philip sweetness,' she whispered huskily. 'Such things you do to me. I have never felt like this before.' Her small hands gave him an affectionate tug. 'I'm glad your company sent you back to represent it at the exhibition.' Apart from a slight accent her English was perfect. 'I missed you, Mr Foot.'

'For three days?' he asked with modest incredulity.

'You devil, you are teasing me. You know three days can be an eternity, yes? You have been on my mind ever since we met. Now this . . . this collision, yes? At last.'

She made it sound as if the three days had been three aeons at least. Aided and abetted by her husky voice, it was good mood-inducing dialogue. And he did not have to guess what mood.

'You have a marvellous ability to obsess a man's mind.'

'Have you thought of me?'

'Do you imagine I have bothered to think of anything except you?'

Her grateful smile as they collided again suggested she had spent her entire life until this fateful mutual recognition waiting for him to arrive to say such words.

Visually she was considerably more than a woman with a superb physique. She was gorgeous. Both her curled thick hair of unassisted dark gold and large cornflower blue eyes told of superb health. So did the fine-grained skin of her suntanned neck and arms; there was nothing even remotely hinting at a wrinkle. Her legs were strong and shapely. Although tall, her feet were small. Absolutely nothing about her appearance could let anyone mistake her for 'the little woman'. Every male below a couple of hundred years old would realise at sight that the erect body under the simple white linen miniskirt and dull blue silk blouse with its wide collar was generous and proportionate; he was in an excellent position to know. Most people would take her for nearer thirty-five than forty-something. Indeed she provided striking evidence that many mature women had advantages over their younger sisters.

She had told Silk that she was Marie Czernin and came originally from the German-speaking Swiss town of Vermala in Bern canton. Their first meeting had been casual enough. A German official merely brought her up, saying they should get to know each other, two weeks ago at an exhibition of British products where Silk was one of a team of four representatives of a new company producing computers. She attended the show, she told Silk, because she was a free-lance journalist. After that first encounter he had taken her out to dine at a Hungarian restaurant full of candlelight and tzigane music and sweatily costumed waiters, went swimming with her at one of the newest luxury pools, and then took her to a Beethoven concert at the Philharmonic and on to one of the wilder nightclubs on the evening prior to his brief return to London.

At the Hungarian restaurant she had confided that she was once married to a Belgian with exotic sexual habits who deserted her for a woman who shared his hobby. Since then she had never used his name though two or three years had elapsed until the divorce due to some technicalities she never understood. She referred to him as 'my little Belgian'. At the nightclub, over a glass of vodka, her favourite drink, she had confided how men of every variety pestered her since she became a lone woman but she preferred to work and retain her independence. Silk had cause to assume himself favoured. When he telephoned her from London twenty-four hours ago to tell her that his firm had decided to send him back she had given every sign of pleasure possible along a telephone line. Her face was radiant when she met him off the airplane at Tempelhof.

As she drew back her head and opened her eyes he saw her smile. This time she did not retreat the sixteenth of an inch. Her eyes conveyed female awareness of a male moving in for the kill. It did not seem to alarm her unduly.

'It is good we have the weekend,' she said huskily; 'we can slouch around and be ourselves. You shall decide what we do.' Her face had the expression of a trusting child. 'I will think of things to please you.'

'Just so long as we are together.'

'I hope you do not flatter every woman like this.'

'Are there other women?'

Abruptly the lift-cage started to descend. They nearly fell, then his hand found the buttons. Marie clung to him while it rose again.

'I feel as if I am floating,' she said in a lost sort of voice.

'It was good vodka.'

She shook her head. 'It wasn't the vodka, darling,' she told him sleepily though he guessed her mind was wide-awake and her senses sharp. As they reached the floor she said: 'Take me home quickly.'

He followed her out of the lift into a long cream and pale grey corridor. With a youthful gesture she caught hold of his hand, laughing softly as if her thoughts excited her. When they turned left into another corridor a man ahead of them was pacing slowly away. He turned swiftly.

No one would call him a beauty. He was thin, of average

height and pointed features. Wings of grey hair flopped over jug ears. Although it was the weekend he wore the white shirt symbolic of the working days; a drab tie held its limp collar together. His pale grey suit fitted nowhere. His black shoes had clearly been retrieved from a dustbin.

He began to abuse Marie in a hissed torrent of German compounds. His voice quivered as if he were about to burst into tears. A frown plucking at her eyebrows indicated well-bred contempt. Her hand kept Silk beside her while she waited for the man to stop or step aside. Instead he drew a deep breath and rushed at Silk, arms flailing.

Silk had no chance to escape.

A less than average-sized fist whipped past his left ear. Simultaneously another fist bounced back off his chest. At once the man jumped back, jigging about like an imitation Cassius Clay. He had already started to run out of breath. His jaw fell open and his nostrils dilated. But he was game. He charged forward again, eager to spoil his rival's handsome features. His evident astonishment at having his wrist caught and wrenched aside wrung a whimper of pain from him. It also ended his desire to fight. Breathing wetly, he allowed himself to be propelled back along the corridor to the lift. Marie followed at a distance.

Silk held him firmly till the cage arrived. Directly it stopped he opened it and shoved the man inside. That individual twisted round, gazing at him with spaniel-sad eyes while he pleaded for compassion—he used the German word *Mitleid*, meaning with grief or sorrow, there being no true equivalent to the English word—and claimed Marie had sworn she was his true woman. Silk shook his head.

'Sorry, I don't speak your language,' he said, and shut the doors.

When the cage started to descend he returned to the tense figure of Marie. Her earlier vivacity had gone and she kept her face averted. While they retraced their steps he put an arm round her.

'Attractive girls like you run risks. You need someone

to take care of you.'

She gave a non-laugh. 'People are too busy to be bothered about an ordinary woman,' she said. 'Women like me mean nothing.'

'Darling, such nonsense.'

She smiled unsurely. Clearly the incident had disturbed her. He kept his arm round her until she stopped outside a plain dove-grey door and opened her bag to hunt through its bric-a-brac for a key-ring.

'This is my little home. Here I can be myself.'

When she had unlocked the door she took his hand again to draw him into a small dark entrance-hall. He shut the door and followed her through a shadowy open doorway and blinked as she switched on the lights.

It took him by surprise. They were in a spacious stone-coloured room which had a quantity of modern red fabric and black iron spindle-legged easy chairs and a divan on a crimson fitted carpet. He had met many elephants who would look small and solitary on the divan. Against the left-hand wall, facing the divan, was the inevitable twentyone-inch colour television box and along the wall above it an enormous oblong mirror. Left of the television was one of the chairs and two iron-grille gates; beyond them, Marie told him, were the two bedrooms, a bathroom and a loo. Right of the television set was the main unit of a stereophonic phonograph and two racks of sleeved discs. On their right were long uncurtained windows in front of which a large oval glass-topped and iron-legged table supported a vast bowl of flame and gold and scarlet carnations and a cheap radio set. In front of the right-hand wall was a well-stocked portable bar, another huge oblong wall mirror, flanked by ornamental vases full of fresh flowers, and a five-foot high open-ironwork screen which turned part of the room into a small separate dining section. Beyond the table and chairs a plain red door led to the kitchen and pantry.

At sight the room had the impersonal unlived-in appearance of a furniture dealer's display. There were no pictures. A row of textbooks between red stone Chinese dragon book-ends on the table in front of the window provided the only literature. It lacked only price-tags for each item. He thought the glass-top table peculiarly untasteful. Everything was untasteful.

'I'm sorry everything is so untidy,' Marie apologized. It sounded like a man apologizing for the one solitary hair on his otherwise bald head. 'I had no chance to do any housework before I came to meet you. My old "wife"—what do you call them? Charladies? Treasures?—my old "wife" decided to give up a few weeks ago. I've been too busy to find a new one.'

'Looks tidy to me.'

'Englishmen are always so considerate.'

She let go of his hand and faced him. Her eyes did not attempt to conceal her worry.

'What must you think?' she asked unhappily. 'That man has ruined our lovely weekend.'

'Attractive girls must expect men to be a nuisance. It's a vocational hazard. He hasn't ruined my weekend.'

She drew a deep breath. 'He told you I am his lover,' she said.

'Good gracious!'

'It is untrue. How could I have anything to do with such a man? He is repulsive to me, a failure, and ill. He has a heart condition. He is Kurt Hagen, a radio reporter. I met him when I went to Bonn to write an article two years ago.'

'You don't have to explain,' he told her bleakly.

'You must understand. Oh, your face is so expressive, Philip. I know what you are feeling. After these lovely times we've had together . . . I was so happy just sitting there having dinner with you . . . you must listen.'

'This is painful for you. I'd better go.'

'No!' she exclaimed. 'No.' Her right hand rose as if to reach out to him and fell to her side. 'It will spoil more than this weekend unless you listen and try to believe me . . . Kurt is lonely. He's sad. He has what the Germans call *Weltschmerz,* world pain, a sickness of life. No woman wants him.' Her voice had an earnest note. 'I tried to help him.'

'You are too kind.'

'He has never been here although he is always pleading.'

Silk hesitated as if just aware that someone had tipped a tray of ice-cubes among his pleasantly warming thoughts.

'Other men have wanted you,' he said roughly.

She gave no sign of resentment at his tone. Her eyes were candid.

'Only a few, Philip. I have always been fastidious. I prefer to be alone . . . shall I tell you about those who have wanted me?'

'It is nothing to do with me.'

Marie reacted oddly. 'Don't say that, Philip,' she said meekly, like a woman too proud to plead. 'This has been a very happy evening for me. Such evenings are rare.' Her modest tone and hurt eyes never wavered. 'Kurt Hagen never meant anything to me. Can you understand?'

After a pause Silk nodded. 'I think so,' he answered in an easier tone. 'You are too warm-hearted. It never pays. Will this individual come back tonight?'

'He may.'

'He has done so on other occasions.'

'Yes.'

He looked round the room. 'Well,' he said finally, 'I'd better stay for a bit. If you would like me to.'

Immediately her face regained its capacity for vivacity. She nodded and then, impulsively, moved forward and gave a sigh of relief as he took her in his arms. When she raised a tautly smiling face her eyes were shut. Her lips twisted weakly under his. A moan strained in her throat. Abruptly she wrenched herself free, smiling unsteadily. Her eyes were unhappy again.

'Philip, we must be sensible.'

'Oh nonsense.'

'No yes, yes I must be though you make it hard for me,' she said. 'Nothing must spoil our weekend. I feel too close to you to let any misunderstanding harm our friendship.' She stepped back a pace, smiling worriedly, her hands clasping and unclasping. 'It's stuffy in here. Take off your Jacket. Shall I open a window?'

'Good idea.'

As she opened one of the windows he took off his jacket and tossed it on to one of the theatrical chairs. She came back and loosened his tie and undid the collar of his shirt.

'Would you like a drink? I have vodka and cognac and English gin.'

'As I'm waiting for Hagen I'd better have coffee if there is any. I might relax too much if I had another drink. He might knock me out cold.'

She laughed incredulously. 'He is too sick to fight anyone,' she said. 'I'd like coffee too. But I've only got the instant sort.'

'Fair enough . . . ah, I've had an idea. Let me get it while you relax. Or have you a thing against people using your kitchen?'

'You are not people. You'll find everything easily. I'll make myself comfortable.'

She smiled, still unsurely, and went through the quaint gates to the bedrooms.

Silk wandered over to the table. A glance proved the books were indeed for reference plus the usual notebooks and scribble pad and address-lists which a journalist keeps near the telephone. Looking round, feeling like a stage designer inspecting a new set, he wandered past the empty dining-table and chairs and let himself into the kitchen. He switched on the light.

Unlike most apartment kitchens, you could have swung a cat in it. No doubt practical German wives insisted on a decent-sized kitchen and refused to put up with the cubicle no larger than a ship's galley which male domestic architects elsewhere thought ample. Most of what he saw was white with enamel gadgetry which reduced toil, plus touches of red like the linoleum and the handles of kitchenware. A steel sink and draining-boards ran alongside long windows with red curtains.

He found the crockery and borrowed a cup and went to the sink. There he washed out his mouth. After several minutes the sour taste still lingered; it was probably psychological. A hunt through the pantry produced a packet of Italian biscuits, from the Milan people; a pleasant bonus.

When he had made and poured the coffee into gold-banded white mugs he unzipped his small fob pocket and took out a short strip of cellophane wrapper containing two tiny pills. He split the wrapper open, dropped the pills into one mug, turned over the spoon alongside it, put the cellophane back into his fob pocket and rezipped it. Finally he surveyed the tray to ensure it held everything required, and carried it into the livingroom.

Marie had not returned. A draft of warm air from the open window provided a bonus of petrol fumes and tangled noises from people who were still not asleep. He put the tray down on the enormous divan with the mug beside the overturned spoon nearest the wall. Then he went to the window and shut out the smells and sounds of the city. Back at the divan he righted the spoon and added sugar to the other mug and drank most of the coffee in it. As he put down the mug he called to her. An answer assured him she was just coming. He straightened, legs apart, the virile male with no problems on his tiny mind. His trial smile would have caused the rising sun to sink back over the horizon from sheer chagrin.

'Darling, here I am.'

She had a flair for entrances. In the interval she had changed into a little thing of stiffly rustling black figured silk with a deep silver collar which clasped her neck like a manacle and broad silver braid down the corsage. It had voluminous Tudor sleeves and a flared skirt which swept the floor. She had tidied her shining gold hair and used a strong perfume. He noted that her lips were undressed. She smiled pleasedly at the expression in his eyes and, with a return of her former spontaneity, ran to him and put her arms round him.

'I like feeling you against me. It is nice, yes?'

'Gorgeous.'

'You are so flat, such strong muscles.'

'You don't mind if I prefer your front to mine, do you? Shall we sit down? We're having coffee, remember? I left it to you to add sugar.'

'I don't want coffee. I want to stay here, feeling you against me.'

'After I've slaved over a hot stove since you left me?'

She laughed. 'We had better drink coffee or you'll get cross with me,' she said. 'Kiss me first.'

She clung tightly. Her trembling implied that he had a powerful effect on her. It took him less than one second to realise that under the dramatic robe she was naked.

When she drew her head back she held onto him and kept her face raised. A dreamy expression smoothed her lovely face. Reluctantly she opened her eyes, smiling at him, and then sat down and had a taste of his sweetened coffee before, without adding sugar or milk, she drank most of what was in her mug. Still holding it, she half-turned to prop herself against him. She gave another fond laugh as his hand moved over her gown.

'This is so good,' she said in a humble tone, and sipped coffee. 'It is wonderful to have you here. You would be very conceited if you knew what I have been thinking about you.'

'How could I be? I know I'm terribly handsome and intelligent.'

'You are laughing at me. I mean it.'

'Be a good girl and finish your coffee.'

She did so like a child trying to please someone. As she put the mug down on the tray he threaded his fingers into her hair and hauled her back across his chest. Supported by his arm, she rested her head against his shoulders with her eyes already closed and her lips smiling. While he gazed on her face he felt her fingers undo buttons of his shirt and her bare arm slid inside and coiled around his ribs. When his mouth met hers it was open and her tongue leapt to meet his. Her nails dragged across his skin.

When he let go of her she fell across his legs. She kept her eyes closed and a languid smile softened her damp lips. Lazily she raised her left arm, her fingers twiddling in search of his shoulder until she found it and half-lifted herself to wind it round his neck. 'Take me to bed,' she muttered huskily. 'Carry me. I left the light on.'

He found it a good thing he had given up most weakening habits. His arms discovered she was a splendid bundle of woman to lift around but he accomplished the journey without mishap and laid her down on the wide bed. As he commenced to straighten she clutched at him, frowning when he told her he had to fetch his jacket. Back in the livingroom he took his time over carrying the tray of crockery to the kitchen and flushing the mugs with hot water. He also washed his mouth out again, without noticeable benefit. Finally he collected his jacket and went to admire the plumbing.

When he entered the bedroom she lay naked on the bed watching the doorway and the housecoat trailed untidily across the gold-tinted carpet. He had not seen her naked before. A strain about her eyes suggested she had found it hard to wait for him. She beckoned impatiently. He tossed his jacket onto an easy chair and sat down on the bed, smiling at her. Immediately she caught hold of him and pulled him over her. Her mouth sought his.

Within one minute the strength went from her hands and her mouth lost urgency. He let another two minutes die. As he straightened up her arms seemed to slide off him. She breathed steadily. Just to be sure he laid his hand over her heart and then took her pulse. When he raised one eyelid she remained unaware of the delights her eye was missing. Reassured, he shut her eye. She should be out for six hours at least. As an additional safeguard he kissed her mouth fiercely. There was no response.

He got up and went round the characterless room on a

careful search. It took nearly twenty minutes to ensure no bug relayed voices here to any distant listener. Each time he glanced at Marie she was still unconscious. He got one of his fountain-pens from his jacket and loosened the cap.

'All clear,' he said.

While he waited for the doorbell to ring he stood looking down at her.

2

Silk shook his head.

His unconscious companion was a much-used woman.

Her name had never been Marie Czernin. She had been born Helga Pohl. She was not Swiss. Although she sheared time off her age, she was born forty-three years ago at Annaburg in what was now East Germany, the third daughter of a well-respected family of merchants. This meant her childhood was spent in the sinister decadence of the between-wars period when, rightly or wrongly, many Germans felt humiliated by defeat in the first war and by terms of the armistice imposed on them, when the death of a million men and the maiming of hundreds of thousands caused widespread lesbianism, and homosexuality among men who found themselves derided by many women, when the whole country was a vast jungle where personal survival dominated every activity, where the smells of fear and corruption were everywhere for children to breathe. Helga and her sisters were loyal *Narzissen*, female Nazis. They tossed flowers at the Führer and stones at the Annaburg Jews.

At seventeen Helga married a young soldier, Wolfgang Schlier. Two weeks later he was sent to the Eastern Front. War conditions following her childhood environment soon revealed her emotional imbalance. A week after Wolfgang departed the first of many junior officers became her lover. Seven months later she discovered herself to be pregnant. A back-street abortion affected her health for months. During her convalescence Wolfgang was killed during a Russian attack.

Soon afterwards Helga had commenced work as a journalist in the north German port of Rostock. She was there, living with another of her short-term lovers, when for the second time in less than thirty years Germany was militarily defeated. She left Rostock only hours before Russian troops stormed into it. After some days she reached Berlin and went on to the battered city of Cologne, where she obtained work with a newsagency. At that time another generation of young German women faced an unsure future. In large bombed cities they outnumbered men by three to one; their present and future plight caused widespread social problems. As if anticipating suspicion from the Occupying Powers Helga had already claimed to be Swiss and Marie Czernin and that her parents had died in an air-raid during a wartime visit to Berlin. This gave her the best of both worlds. It ensured German sympathy while separating her from German girls, which, according to OP brasshats, made her friendships with Western soldiers more or less innocuous.

Her natural facility with languages helped her to learn English quickly. On an assignment to Belgium she renewed her acquaintance with Guy Cammaerts, a Brussels newspaperman whom she met first soon after she reached Cologne. Within three weeks she had married him; it was believed she had failed to persuade a senior British officer to marry her and she chose Cammaerts whom she knew to be easy-going, impressionable, and easily led, particularly by a woman with her guile. Her determination took them to London as correspondents for his newspaper and her agency. Within a few months she had left him though according to her own story they remained together for several years. At that time she reverted to using the name of Czernin.

In London she lived with her first known 'wife'. Little evidence of this woman had remained. She was known to be wealthy, nearly fifty, stout and plain, without much education or intelligence, and given to weeping into her gin at the local pub. But she could cook and do housework, was bedazzled by Helga's Continental charm, and had money to lavish on her. Some months later a similar woman, with more money and some years younger, appeared on the scene. One evening the first 'wife' wept more copiously into her gin. Nobody ever saw her again. Soon afterwards Helga set up house with her new 'wife' in Swiss Cottage.

Early the following year she did everything possible to persuade a wealthy American colonel to marry her. He was too wily to fall for her charms; he had been married three times. Simultaneously her second 'wife' discovered a new love and left Swiss Cottage without prior notice one day while Helga was collecting a story in the Midlands.

According to available evidence her hatred of the West dated from that time. A British officer had failed to give into her; an American had also failed to do what she wanted; a 'wife' had shown her that even her female relationships were not to be severed only by her decision.

She had gone to Cologne on holiday. There was evidence that she visited her parents in Annaburg. She had not seen either of her sisters; one had married an Italian and lived in Turin, the other was married to a Canadian and lived in Toronto and never communicated with her family. Then she disappeared from known records for nearly a month. Suddenly she reappeared in London. It was believed that she became an agent for East Germany at this time and was taken over by the KGB soon afterwards. From this time her male companions were all impressable young Civil Servants and politicians amazed by their own brilliance and magnificent futures.

Obviously she completely satisfied her East German spymasters, the Main Intelligence Administration, HVA, a sub-division of the Ministry of State Security, the MfS, the section which conducted subversion against NATO and the West.

On its instructions Helga had applied for a vacant position with her newsagency in Berlin. Later evidence suggested her transfer was ordered by a personal assistant of Lieutenant-General Miekle, head of East German Intelligence in the political sphere.

Within weeks of being given the post Helga had established herself.

This crowded virile noisy narrow arena proved an admirable stage for her talents and indulgences. Unlike the sick Maria Knuth, who became head of the East German Ring Kolberg here while dying of cancer, she had been given no training in operating radio transmitters, in coding and decoding, or other espionage skills. She ran her ring under the guise of a woman journalist who indulged her passion for men as she chose. Her main task was to contact Britons and Americans chosen for her by a HVA administrator.

Helga had done well. There was Albertson, an American ballistics expert in Berlin on vacation after attending an international conference. There was White, a British officer acting as a highly placed NATO official, a widower and lonely. After friendships of four or five months, during which time both men had confided some of their professional secrets to her, they had been mown down and killed by hit-and-run drivers after leaving her flat.

Her most conspicuously successful service to her masters was her ability to strike up an acquaintance with visiting British businessmen. There was something strange about her skill in choosing those whose position and type of product gave them additional significance for Russians. Several of them had accepted her invitation to use her flat as an office on their visits to Berlin and their business telephone conversations had been secretly taped. Two of them experienced awkward interviews when it became known that East German electronic companies were marketing items only slightly different from their own products. Both admitted to having been her lovers and agreed that her performance in bed was vastly unlike what they experienced at home; a more forthright individual had described her as 'a Casaneva of the decade of orgasmic obsession'.

As a result Helga's background had been given a depth examination by the West German Verfassungsschutz and its British equivalent MI 5. That was when they discovered Albertson and White were killed after leaving her flat.

One week later Giles Priest lunched Silk at one of those Victorian-style clubs where every waiter looked as if he remembered the Boer War more clearly than the last order given him for grilled Dover sole.

'Do you enjoy being back in Britain?' Priest had asked over their coffee.

'I've known it in quieter moods. Still, what could be more inspiring than the sight of brave puddeny politicians pottering in circles like the Christmas staff dance crocodile and claiming they are on a crusade.'

'I saw you took a lot of salt with your lunch.'

'Oh, it isn't only darling Malcolm and darling Noël who can pour the stuff out.'

'How is Fathiya?'

They were interrupted by a quavery voice behind Silk which asked: 'Would you and your guest like a liqueur, my lord?'

Priest looked at his guest, and shook his head. 'Not today, thank you, Findley,' he answered.

'Thank you, my lord,' quavered the voice.

'I haven't seen Fathiya since I got back,' Silk replied. 'I read she is on holiday in the south of France.'

'I heard she spent two weeks at her old home in Alexandria. Of course, Nassah couldn't keep her there. It would create an international scandal even though she is Egyptian. It's a good thing all her millions in oil are not involved in the present Middle East situation.'

'Yes.'

'Will you be seeing her?'

'I doubt it.'

'She would like to see you.'

Silk saw no reason to answer questions about a private matter concerning the one woman he did not want to have involved with him publicly. It could be extremely dangerous for her. At present the Arab temperament was sniffing about for enemies everywhere and to hell with whoever got in its way.

'That's decent of her,' he said cheerfully. 'Foolish girl.'

'Are you free for the next few weeks?'

'I am often free since the government, our beloved government, decided on its west of Scillies policy.'

Priest laughed tolerantly. 'I bought that one,' he admitted. 'How about a little trip to Moscow?'

'Alone?'

'Yes.'

'Mmmm. Mmmm. My dear friend. Yes. A game of Russian roulette, yes? Actually, I'm rather dear to me. I can think of cosier things than growing a beard and starving in Lubyanka. But umm go ahead.'

'One of our Russian specialists, Julian Monkman, is an admirer of your work in the Middle East.'

'You've still got intelligent men there then. Am I allowed to take one luxury?'

'No weapon. Only a poison pill. And I'd want you to undertake a small job for me in Berlin first. No one else would know about it. The West German people have asked me to do a task which needs some subtlety.'

'This,' Silk said, 'begins to sound like the Chesterton poem about the rolling English drunkard and the rolling English road. How does it end? "For there is good news yet to hear and fine things to be seen, before we go to Paradise by way of Kensal Green." What is this about?'

Priest glanced round to ensure no one could overhear them. He pushed his empty coffee-cup aside and rested his elbows on the table.

'Are you still interested in the Middle Eastern area?' he asked quietly.

Silk studied him thoughtfully. 'I did live there for

several years until the government started to bawl "stop the world, we want to get off",' he said. 'More.'

'You know about these Russian generals being murdered by the KGB.'

'I've heard rumours.'

'You've read about the purge of intellectuals.'

'Yes.'

'Primakov praised your knowledge of Russian.'

'Civil of him.'

Priest glanced round again. 'We know a Russian naval officer opposed to Brezhnev and his plan to dominate the Mediterranean area,' he resumed. 'He knows the present Russian sub strength. It constitutes the biggest threat Europe has ever known and is aimed to starve Britain into accepting a revolution by preventing contact with the States. He has details of the scheduled naval construction programme and plans for strategic displacement in the Med and Western Approaches.'

Silk scratched his chin. 'Primakov and I had several talks,' he recalled. 'He had a cousin who was a navy man . . . Feodor Strelnikov? A widower. Childless.'

'Oh?'

'What else?'

'There is also a social scientist who heads one cell of intellectual disaffectionists who can tell us who has been executed and poisoned.'

'Quite a package. Where does Berlin come into it?'

'That is my idea,' Priest answered. 'Whoever goes must have a cover. We have a friend in a new computor company who can give our man a crash course as a salesman in ten days. His company has a stand at a Berlin exhibition next month. It would provide a chance to get the spiel right.' He hesitated. 'Berlin has a complication.'

After a long pause Silk asked: 'Do you hear me bating my breath?'

Priest gave a non-smile. 'It may be an unpleasant chore,' he said as if confessing to something. 'It involves a woman. Not a nice type. Devious, vain, ruthless, an occasional lesbian, an all-time nymph, with a great ability to play the brave little woman. And a congenital liar.'

'Is that all?'

'More or less.'

'British?'

'No,' Priest had replied and told him about White and Albertson. He hesitated. 'We can arrange for her to meet you. What happens then is up to you . . . but there is Fathiya. And how you feel.'

'Yes,' Silk agreed, and rubbed his stomach. 'When you see Fathiya remember me to her. Have you a dossier on this charmer?'

At that point Priest had stood up. 'Come along to my office,' he had said. 'We can take a taxi. I've given up bringing the car to town. If you meet Monkman or any of the others don't mention this Berlin matter to them. It does not involve them.'

And as he stood looking down at her limp sprawl he thought she differed little from many nude female Caucasians. Physiologically, her worst feature were her patellas, large as half-bricks, and, in repose, her mandible was very heavy. Still, these were minor blemishes in an otherwise attractive woman.

How had Nietzsche put it? ' "*Ein Hunger wachst aus meiner Schönheit: wehe tun möchte ich denen, welchen ich leuchte, berauben möchte ich meine Beschenkten: also hungere ich nach Bosheit*",' he muttered. 'Something like that . . . "A hunger grows out of my beauty: I would rather hurt those upon whom I shine, rob those to whom I have given myself: thus do I hunger after malice." ' He nodded. 'Something like that, old girl?'

As the doorbell chimed he caressed her shoulder. There was no response. He drew the rose-coloured sheet up to her neck.

Warm air from the open transom window curled round his neck as he left the room. He crossed the livingroom to the small hallway and opened the door to admit the two men outside. With that action he ended his original task, to admit West German officials into the flat without disturbing any booby-trap which could have put her on her guard. They were after more significant game than one treacherous woman.

Without a word the two men entered. One was small inside his grey suit and pale blue shirt. A dark wiry stubble sprouted round his chin; an ancient grey hat was tilted back from his sweat-shiny forehead. He bore some similarity to a Christmas tree on account of the quantity of photographic equipment hung around him. His name was Max Felfe. His companion was Kurt Hagen. No emotional distress showed on his face now. On the contrary he radiated authority. His name was Hans Schnitter and he was an agent of the Verfassungsschutz.

As Silk shut the door Schnitter looked at him solicitously. 'I did not hurt you, Herr Foot, no?' he said. 'I hit you harder on the chest than I intended, you understand, yes?'

'I'll live awhile,' Silk prophesied and led them into the livingroom.

They glanced round with interest unharmed by envy. Schnitter nodded.

'So,' he said approvingly. 'We a long time agree she an Englishman in would allow if he appeared a soft fool, yes, she could with a little fondle cheat, yes? Where the bedroom is?'

His English crackled and jerked like a faulty buzz-saw.

'Here.'

Silk led them into the bedroom. They looked at Marie without interest. Schnitter appeared to be searching for words. When he found them he kept his voice down.

'Such women have we few in Germany, *danke Gott*. They are not, how do you say, please? *gebrauchlich*?'

'Usual?' Silk suggested, and helped everyone by switching to German. 'No, I'm sure she is not usual. It might be interesting to know why she became what she is.'

Schnitter raised his brows incredulously. 'Englishmen

love to find reasons for everything,' he said. 'It must be a national hobby. Such women exist. Human nature is seldom motivated by logic, mostly by emotion. There are unhappy millionaires and contented tramps. This woman is a female sewer rat.'

'Ah,' Silk said, and glanced at the bed. 'I'll search this room. If she should come to, I'm the one she expects to find here.'

3

An hour later they started to photograph the material they had unearthed from various places and stacked on the glass table. Evidently no one had warned her against carelessness. She was a compulsive letter-hoarder. One discovery was a bundle of nearly forty torrid love-letters from a West German government official, each neatly dated in her handwriting. She had also kept some indiscreet letters from the Briton and American who were killed after leaving her.

Schnitter and Felfe were particularly excited by letters from someone who signed himself Franz. On one her tidy pen had written an East Berlin address.

Silk had discovered two significant items. One could raise fascinating legal points and the other filled him with foreboding. A licence issued by a London registrar's office claimed that a Helga Cammaerts of Brussels had married one Clark Alfred Fortescue Jonathan Denning, a British subject, of Marlborough Mansions, St Marylebone. Unless his memory had cheated him, it was issued about a month after she returned to London from her visit to East Germany. He suspended judgment on it; the licence could easily be a forgery. Unquestionably the second item had greater significance. It was a carbon copy of a recent letter she had sent to Franz and gave the names of people in a cell of Russian intellectual disaffectionists in Moscow headed by a Professor Konuzin. She had told Franz that the list had come from Jeremy in London a few days ago.

While the Germans photographed other material he wondered how she received the information from London. They had failed to locate any codes or ciphers: a city *femme fatale* like Marie seldom had the wits to master such complications. Her current diary was a small thin book with a week to every two facing pages, allowing sufficient space for random jottings and a variety of male given names with an evening date against each; Jeremy did not appear among them.

On a sudden inspiration he went into the bedroom. Since his last visit Marie had turned onto her front and pushed down the sheet, a static pink wave over her thighs. She breathed so evenly that scarcely any movement showed in her long flawless back.

He watched her for a moment and then went to the chest-of-drawers in which he had already replaced her older diaries. He sat down beside her to leaf through those for the last four years. At once he found one feature which assumed new significance. At irregular intervals each of them had some days, usually three or four together though on one occasion they reached a full week, which contained no *memoire d'amour* entry. Instead each had L on the first day and either the next day or the one after the letter J. That was all. Her next entries related to a male meal-ticket. Sometimes there were single sentence expressions of delight as if she expected to live to be a very old woman who would need memories to warm her.

He frowned at the empty space. They implied such an obvious pattern that he distrusted it. They could cover days when she had gone to London or Lisbon and met Jeremy who had given her information to pass to Franz for transmission to Moscow. His mind rejected such a simple explanation. His entire training told him that the letters must have a more abstruse significance. Nothing in espionage ever provided such an easy solution. Still frowning he put the diaries in sequence and got up and replaced them in the chest-of-drawers. As he did so he heard her moan, a meaningless sigh in her throat, and she muttered *liebchen liebchen* without waking. After a moment she began to breathe steadily again.

He hovered at the foot of the bed until he was fairly sure she would not wake. Then he rejoined the other men. They had nearly finished. Felfe was replacing various documents where he had found them.

'We should get something positive from tonight's work,' Schnitter said cheerfully. 'We have much to work on. Something may tell us where she banks most of the money they pay her. You are also satisfied?'

'I have some leads.'

As they prepared to leave they had a final look round to be sure they had left no trace of their visit. At the door Silk turned to Schnitter.

'Don't forget to call me at quarter to seven. She should be almost awake by then.'

Schnitter nodded. 'One of our men will call,' he promised. 'He will say he is ringing from your hotel. Mr Stewart, an executive of your company, arrived last night and wants to see you before he flies to Istanbul and can you return quickly. Yes?'

'Your man is to say he is the hotel telephonist and mislaid the number I gave him where he could get me.'

'Ah so. Thank you for your cooperation. It is good she has a weakness for Englishmen, yes?'

'You think so?'

Silk shut them out and wandered round the flat to reassure himself there were no signs which could awaken her suspicion. It was an hour for the perfectionist to indulge himself. He need not have worried: Schnitter and Felfe were both highly trained operators, skilled products of General Gehlen's training methods. Then he returned to the bedroom.

Once again she had changed position, turned onto her back and gone down into the bed with her arms folded above her head. He undressed tidily. Scratching roundabout he sat down and studied her placid face.

'What can I do to get you to talk to me about Jeremy?' he whispered.

After some minutes he stretched out alongside her to think.

He partly awoke as an unmistakably female warmth stirred against him. Weak lips found his neck appetizing. An errant hand wandered over him. He had a lively suspicion that someone was trying to take advantage of him.

He produced a drowsy sound to imply pleasure. He really should have known better. Instantly the lips honouring his gorgeous neck became more purposeful and the hand tenderly outrageous. With an effort he freed his left arm and raised it to see his watch. It was nearly half-past seven. Prickles of alarm went along his nerves. For the life of him he saw no logical excuse for an abrupt unilateral termination of such comforts as were his right now. A lover did not unpin himself from an ardent woman at crack of dawn on Sunday to brush his teeth or fret about the stock market. To the best of his recollection the *Scout's Handbook* had no advice on the matter.

Her muffled voice asked if he was awake. He saw a wing of her gold hair spilled over his chest. Her hand was affectionate and proprietorial.

'No,' he said.

She trembled with silent laughter and asked if he had enjoyed himself.

'Ja, schon. Was fur dich?'

'Ah ja, mein Liebster, wunderbar,' she muttered huskily. She eased slowly up along his body to give his senses a treat and kissed his lips.

'Liebst' Liebst',' she muttered unsteadily. *'O Gott, Ich habe dich so lieb, ja so lieb . . .'* His query brought a drowsy affirmation: *'Gott ja, du mein Liebhaber, es ist unertraglich, Herzliebster, es geht mir gut . . .'*

Her thick tone and unsure grammer told him that she

was not as awake as he had feared. 'Go to sleep,' he muttered on a faked yawn, and within seconds she fell asleep in his arms. It took some while to untangle himself without waking her. When he finally got off the bed she was still on holiday. He looked at his watch again. It was nearly quarter to eight.

Something had gone wrong. He was afraid of what it could be.

Soon after nine o'clock he carried a breakfast tray into the bedroom. Since leaving it he had bathed and she had awakened. She lay uncovered, arms stretched out on either side, lips smiling, a collector's sheen in her eyes. From her attitude he gathered she was convinced he now had a fair knowledge of her as a woman. A quiver went through her as she saw a gleam in his eyes. As he heeled the door shut she sat up, yawning, smoothed hair back from her face, and stretched her arms high above her head. Seen like this, with sunlight sliding about her tanned body and limbs, he did not wonder that many men had found her attractive. Beyond question she was a magnificent animal to see and if sight was a true guide she was superbly healthy and had the stamina of ten navvies. She was also less introverted than the bint coyly arisen from a shell in Botticelli's *Birth of Venus*. Her hands did not flutter about in sham modesty. He put the tray on the bed.

'Darling, it's wonderful to see you here just as I've imagined it,' she exclaimed, and glanced at the tray. 'Perfect!' She laughed gaily. 'Can you cook too? You would make an excellent wife.'

'I'm better at being just a hovering pretty face.'

'That is British humour. You are much more. Very handsome, but more.'

'Stop dreaming and eat your croissant while it's hot.'

'How I envy all those glamourous women you have known.'

'Blossoms borne away on the stream of life,' he said casually.

'Please, I am being serious. You are a wonderful lover. So strong, *schon oh schon*, you understand? I never felt like this before. You have made me feel like a girl at the commencement of life.'

'Just so your time wasn't wasted.'

'Such stamina! I had not expected it.'

'I go in for weight-lifting.'

'I watched you for a long time after you finally went to sleep. You looked like a boy.'

'I know, the haggard lines had gone.'

'Why did you get dressed?' she asked in a petulant tone. 'It is Sunday. We need not hurry.' Her eyes gleamed at him. 'Also, I want you. Do you want me?'

He lowered his cup of coffee to let her see his appreciative gaze travel over her face and down her body. 'Do you think any man in his right senses could ever not want you?' he asked thickly, and shook his head slowly. 'I have to go to my hotel to see if there are any messages.'

She eyed him sullenly. 'Use my telephone,' she said, and her face brightened. 'If there are no messages for you to attend to, we can stay here till we go out for dinner tonight. When you come again you must stay here with me and use the flat as your hotel and office. It will be easier for you. And we can be together at night if you want me.'

Silk replaced his cup in the saucer reluctantly. It was one of those mornings when he needed quarts of coffee to get his brain ticking over. It was one of those mornings when he was not going to get the coffee he needed. Instead he moved closer and seized her in his arms and shoved her head back and kissed her lips and eyes and neck and ears with an enthusiasm which gratified her and satisfied him. She writhed to let his hands gather what she assumed were renewed memories and longing based on knowledge. Then he held her gently and kissed her lips reverently.

'You are a very special woman,' he told her, 'a marvellous woman, a witch, adorable, and beautifully sensual.

There is nothing I would sooner do than stay away from the hotel. But I must go. This once. Next time it will be different. We will stay here together. For a week if you like.'

She sighed unhappily. 'Very well,' she agreed miserably. 'You are right about my being a sensual woman. I love the smell of your body. Come and talk to me while I have a bath. Oh darling, I love you.'

He felt rather sick and smiled at her.

'I do admire men who can be strong-willed,' she said tolerantly and raised her face. 'Kiss me.'

'Don't tempt me too far,' he said after a moment, 'or I won't want to go to my hotel at all.'

He drove them directly to his hotel near the Allied Control building.

When he had bought her a drink he left her reading a magazine in the entrance lounge and went to the reception desk to enquire for messages. There was only one. It had been received less than twenty minutes ago and asked him to ring a name he knew to be a code. As he turned away down a well-lit corridor to a nest of telephone booths his smiling face equalled the alarm of men who could not acknowledge awareness of trouble.

He had no difficulty in getting through to the number given him when he first arrived. All telephone lines in the booths were automatic and did not pass through a switchboard. It took longer to go through the recognition patter to prove his identity. At the far end a fluent voice grated English.

At length it said: 'You may be in danger.'

'Oh?'

'We discovered the body of Herr Schnitter in a dust-bin in Kreuzberg two hours ago. He had been strangled. There was no information about Herr Felfe who is also disappeared.'

'They had a large number of photographs.'

'Nothing has been found. Two men unknown to us

entered the block where the woman has the apartment. This was shortly after you had left. They obviously saw you leave together. You also have photographs?'

'No. I saw the letters and diaries being photographed.'

'This woman is with you?'

'Yes.'

After some other exchanges, equally unimportant, he replaced the receiver but as he hastened into the lounge, with one woman standing beside a nest of luggage, uniformed porters loitering nearby, two girl receptionists at the desk, a man reading a newspaper and a trio of Frenchwomen exclaiming over a floral wall display, he feared that he might be too late already.

Two men held Marie firmly between them and were already halfway to the glass swing-doors. They were half-carrying her so that her feet seemed to skim over the floor. Each man was large and solid, as if he had been born in a *bierkeller*. Thirty-odd years ago their Pappas had probably tarted themselves up in Hitlerian costume; they wore white shirts and pale grey trousers as if it constituted a uniform. Their happy laughter lent the scene a Hitchcockian atmosphere.

4

Silk covered forty-odd yards of carpet and marble at a speed which attracted attention and finished up in front of the trio. One glance told him that Marie was desperately frightened. She seemed to have lost control of her face. Each feature had become separate, no longer part of a whole, and her tan resembled old varnish. Her eyes had the glazed unreality of someone about to faint. Another brief glance told him that the front of the two men was exactly what their rears had forecast: fleshy, jowly, fat above and below small eyes, and stomachs like footballs. Their change of expression at the sight of himself suggested he was as welcome as a bomb on a Christmas tree. One had narrow lips which vanished suddenly and the other had thick lips which clamped together like something in a do-it-yourself kit. Silk knew himself unloved. They faltered in their stride and halted.

He chose the dramatic approach. 'What the hell are you men doing with this lady?' he bellowed furiously. 'Who the devil are you? Let go of her! Do you hear me? Let go of her!'

A silence settled over the lobby. People turned and eyes swivelled. In a hush of expectancy people took on the quality of statues: there was nothing like a chance of seeing a doorstep murder to gain passive attention.

That seemed to unnerve the two men. Perhaps his sudden appearance and raving voice helped. He pushed it along by letting his face tell them that he was one of those customers who went berserk directly he lost his temper. One of them, the now completely lipless man on Marie's right, let go of her and clenched his fists. He dived forward. That was a double error. Everyone saw Marie crumple at the knees and begin to fall. His fists hit Silk without noticeable harm. One blow on his ear sent him staggering. Marie continued to droop slowly, her weight causing the other man to face the problem of whether to support her to the exit or help his friend get rid of the opposition. Suddenly his mind abandoned the effort of deciding which activity promised the safest course. He let go of her and took off past Silk like a sprint champion. His panic upset his comrade. Without warning the latter, sweating and steadying himself, started to breathe sharply down his nose. His arms windmilled wildly. Seconds later he set off after his comrade.

They crashed through the swingdoors without interference.

As Silk helped Marie to stand up the statues came alive. People rushed from all sides to offer assistance. A clatter of tongues like dropped cutlery said their owners had not interfered because they thought it was a scene being recorded for a television play. No one had followed the two men.

'Go away!' Silk snarled at them.

A porter helped him to get Marie up to his room. She said nothing, breathing unsteadily through her open mouth. As he told the man to send up a double cognac and a large Scotch she lay down on the bed. He locked the door, then went over and took off her shoes. She lay rigid. After some moments she folded an arm over her eyes and began to shudder.

He took off his jacket and draped it over a chair beside the window. A scurry of thoughts went through his mind. One thing was clear. This development meant he had to take action on his own initiative. He did not mind that; he could apologize later if anyone protested. But what action? He took off yesterday's shirt and collected a clean one from his suitcase.

'It's going to be another glorious day,' he said, looking out of the window as he unbuttoned the shirt. 'Not a cloud to be seen. And this is the season when our British weather forecasts say future conditions unsettled.'

Marie did not answer. Although she had lowered her arm she was still trembling. In the mirror he saw her gaze flickering around the room.

'I expect the pools will be full all day,' he commented. 'Scarcely surprising. Actually I prefer them when you can swim a few feet without colliding into people. God knows what'll happen if the population explosion continues. I suppose I'll have to get to the nearest pool at about four o'clock in the morning.'

He folded the shirt over the dressingtable chair and went to hunt through his case for a tie.

'My trouble is that I always bring the wrong things away with me. Directly I see what I've brought I wish I'd left out this and brought that.'

He chose a sombre green tie unlikely to offend anyone. Back at the window he put on the clean shirt and unzipped his trousers to smooth its tail around his hips.

'I like watching you move round a bedroom,' Marie said unexpectedly. Her voice was raw and she had trouble over controlling it. 'You are a tidy man without being fussy. All women are untidy. Where did you get those scars?'

'Our very first exhibition was held during a South American revolution. You know about revolutions. If anyone gets in the way the revolutionaries say it was his fault for being there. Ah!'

There was a knock at the door. He went to open it zipping up his trousers and fastening the waist-band. It was the waiter with their drinks.

Silk gave the man a tip and locked the door again. When he took the tray across the room Marie sat up and swung her legs over the edge of the bed. Her sun-tan still had a dingy unreality. An unsteady smile died on her lips.

'You'll feel better after this,' he assured her, and then tossed out an explanation for the incident to see if she would accept it. 'Your friend—what did you say his name is? Hagen? He must have it pretty bad if he can persuade his friends to try to kidnap you.'

He could almost see her mind working as she drank brandy.

She took the opportunity he had provided. 'Poor Kurt,' she said sadly.

'Poor Kurt indeed? Why waste sympathy on him? Are you in love with him?'

She was a great opportunist. This time she seized on the note of jealousy in his voice.

'I pity him,' she replied with commendable womanly gentleness.

'Few women would be so tolerant after such a dreadful experience.'

'It isn't his fault or mine that I affect him this way,' she said modestly. 'A man can be attracted without a woman encouraging him. Kurt is weak. Everyone feels sorry for him. I wish you had not been involved.'

'I'm glad to have been around.'

Her blue eyes grew misty. 'Darling darling Philip, so am

I really!' she exclaimed. 'Oh, I am so lucky to have your friendship. You give me confidence. You know I am not responsible, don't you?'

He switched on his most masculine gleam. 'I saw the type he is,' he commented angrily. 'Shall I ring the police for you?'

She shook her head. 'I'll write him one last appeal to leave me alone,' she said in a tone of simple dignity. 'Please help me with the letter.'

Beyond doubt she had got over her initial shock. No terror showed on her face now. Its expression of sorrow suggested she might soon cry.

'Of course,' he assured her, and walked his drink over to the window to watch toy cars beetle along below while he drank it.

From the metallic yellow sheen creeping across the sky everything hinted that it would be a hot afternoon. A strong smell of petrol exhaust rose from the streets like a sour invisible tide. On such a day, probably on most days, whatever the weather, he doubted if Berliners could ever really get away from each other. On a day like this it was natural for them to be outdoors. They loved physical activities.

He finished his drink slowly.

When he turned Marie lay on the bed with her legs over the side as if ready to jump up to defend herself. Her head was turned away, her eyes closed. She had undone her dress to the waist. Its skirt had ridden up her strong brown thighs. Lipstick stained a balled paper handkerchief beside her hips. He saw that the glass on the bedside table was empty.

'Marie,' he said tentatively.

'Yes, darling.'

'I don't quite know what to do.'

'If we can stay here a little longer I will be all right.'

'No no, it isn't that . . . I have to go back to London.'

That alarmed her. She sat up, turning towards him, her eyes narrowed against the light. 'No!' she exclaimed.

'Why? Oh why?'

He walked over and put his glass down beside hers.

'When I left you downstairs there was a message for me to call our agency representative here immediately. He told me that one of our directors tried to contact me last evening, while we were having dinner, and finally called him to tell me to return today, Something has happened at one of our plants. I don't know what it is but they want me there tomorrow.'

While he spoke she kept on saying God oh God in an anxious tone and her blue eyes filled with fear. It was probably the first time she had not been acting.

'But I've had an idea,' he said in a cheerful voice, and sat down and took her hands in his. Her fingers were cold and unsteady. 'You're busy, I know it, but this has been a nasty experience, so listen to me.'

'What is it?'

He drew her close. 'Darling, come with me,' he pleaded. 'For a few days. A day or two. Longer if you find you can spare the time. Please. It would make me so happy.'

He tried to sound as if she was arguing violently against the idea. Actually she had rested her forehead on his shoulder and said nothing.

Her long silence led him to believe she would refuse. It would scarcely surprise him. They really did write better dialogue for television plays and that was one hell of an admission. She looked up.

'Thank you,' she said. 'It will be a good opportunity to see your home and how you live. I want to share everything with you.'

He kissed her enthusiastically and discovered she was feeling better. 'I'll have lunch sent up here,' he said gaily, 'and then we can collect whatever you want from your flat.'

She shook her head. 'There is no need to go there.' she said. 'I always carry my passport with me. It is an old journalistic habit. We can buy whatever I need at Tempelhof.' She eyed him slyly. 'Do you want me to buy a night-gown?' she whispered.

'You lovely fool!'

She smiled indulgently. 'I shall have you to myself and you will be mine,' she said contentedly. Her voice sharpened. '*Liebchen*, call the airline companies. Oh, this is so romantic. My head is in a whirl. I have never felt like this before. Hurry hurry!'

5

Nothing about Giles Priest tallied with theories of how an espionage director appeared. At close on six feet tall, wearing a well-tailored dark grey suit, a shirt whiter than an angel's wing and the tie of a famous regiment killed off by the present government, he could have been a banker or stockbroker. Everything about his manner was superbly calm and casual on the surface. Absolutely nothing about his appearance suggested that he, the somethingth Lord Esketh, had learned about remote areas of Asia the hard way, astride a pony or on his feet, in the not too distant days when British travellers required a little more adventure than fish and chips on the Costa Brava.

His new office was comfortably furnished without ostentation. Its main colours were dark green and the pale brown of genuine light English oak. A magnificent row of telephones of various colours, including one which was piebald and one skewbald, ranged along his desk. Oak wall panelling which gave no sign of being shields hid the magnificent collection of trickily projected strategic maps. Easy chairs facing wide windows had a magnificent view of sunlit wooded parkland.

While Silk explained what had happened Priest spent most of the time gazing expressionlessly out at the placid sun-bright summer green. He was briefly silent after the account ended. Then he nodded.

'You did quite right,' he commented. 'Just a few questions. Did you have to work hard to persuade her to come here?'

'No.'

'Would she have suggested it if you had not?'

'That's a point . . . I think it's very likely.'

'Could she have picked on you as an excuse for leaving Berlin?'

'I've no means of telling. It's a possibility.'

'You say she was prepared to go quietly with those men. Her nervous exhaustion afterwards suggests she already knew someone in Berlin, presumably East German agents, were suspicious of her.'

'You're saying they suspected her of being a double agent.'

'Correct. They did not know you. They did know Schnitter. Felfe could be known to them or may be an East German agent.'

'Logical,' Silk agreed. 'In which case she intends to hide somewhere here, use me as a bodyguard, and will arrange to vanish while she is at my flat. Sorry, the flat.'

'Money,' Priest said ruminatively after a silence. 'More precisely, the money paid to her by the East Germans and Russians. They obviously paid her in cash. With me?'

'You incline to believe she banked it here in one style or another so that when she had to leave Berlin she would naturally come here.'

'Her record showed she is a professional survivor. Now we're sure she's devious and a flagrant liar.'

'You think she had prepared for this eventuality and her attack of nerves came from fear of being unable to operate her survival plan.'

'Yes.'

'That means she is a double agent.'

'There are other possibilities. She never worked for us.'

Silk watched finches playing hide-and-seek among the trees. 'It could mean she has established another identity here,' he commented. 'If the L in her diary meant London she assumed another identity here. Yes?

'Possibly.'

'It could also mean she left a suitcase somewhere which contained things which would alter her appearance . . . she could take the suitcase on to a long-distance train, change in one of the washrooms, and then, in her disguise, complete the journey in another part of the train.'

'It would be simpler to change her appearance, if she does, at some place where her appearance in either guise does not attract attention.'

'A matter of timing, reaching her destination when nobody was paying attention?'

'Yes.'

'It could be a combination of both. She might believe it safe to vary the pattern.'

Priest nodded. 'At this stage we can only speculate,' he agreed mildly. 'There are two other points. What has happened to this man she presumably married? We should soon know if that certificate is valid. And if she disguises herself and knows Jeremy, does he know her as only one, and if so which one, or as both?' He sat silent for several minutes, staring out of the window. 'I must try to finish the ornamental pool,' he said. 'Tell me more about her. What sort of woman is she? What does she talk about?'

'Herself.'

'Dull. Or isn't it?'

'She's enthralled by it. History began and will end with her.'

'She is reported to like music.'

'That's a line.'

'Books?'

'None. She never has the time.'

'Where did I hear that before? Anything else?'

'A hypochondriac. Pills, potions, vitamin tablets by the ton, everything in Europe to keep her healthy and virile.'

'Anything else?'

Silk hunched his shoulders. 'She's the most extreme

case of narcissism I have encountered,' he said. 'Far worse than most of the show business people I've met who were reputed to qualify for the description.'

'Could it have been due to anxiety?'

'I imagine she took refuge in it from anxiety. From the moment we left Tempelhof we talked solidly about her. I doubt if she ever had any interest outside herself. I'd rank her as a real *Narzisse,* ready to sell anyone and do anything to please and protect herself. Psychologically, she has a formative schizoid imbalance and is a mysophobic.'

'How about the record of her being a nymph?'

'Very probable. It may be only spasmodic now. She loves to imagine herself pursued by every man alive, and, though she's attractive, I doubt if any of them care a hoot except as part of a night on the tiles.'

'Would she blackmail anyone?'

'Most certainly if it suited her.'

Priest nodded and thought for a moment. 'She must have keys,' he said at length.

'She has about twenty. But when we got to the flat and I put her to sleep I found no one had thought of leaving extra cakes of soap. Only one in the bathroom. I'll take some back and get impressions.'

While they had coffee and discussed how to keep Marie under surveillance they were interrupted by a bee-like hum on an upright gadget, rather like a slanted mirror with a deep back and a loudspeaker grille at its base, on the right side of Priest's desk. They got up and walked over. As Priest pressed a stud the screen section, the slanted mirror, came alive. It showed a magnified report from an agent who had traced the marriage certificate. It was genuine. There was no record of a divorce. Denning had left Marlborough Mansions some years ago and had acquired another woman, who was known as his wife. He and the woman, by whom he had two infant sons, lived at Bromley Common. So far as was known he had no political interests. He was employed in the accounts department of an Oxford Street store and appeared to live well beyond his means. Priest pressed another stud which provided voice contact.

'Good,' he said. 'Anything else?'

'He and his family are due to leave on Friday for their holiday. On the Costa Brava. Another family, the Herricks, near neighbours, is going with them. They're driving.'

'Anything else?'

'He bought a Jag XJ6 four months ago. Mrs Denning as she's known drives a secondhand nineteen-sixtysix Cortina to do her shopping.'

'Does he drive to work?'

'No, sir. She takes him to Bromley South station and he has a season ticket.'

'First?'

'No, sir.'

'We'll call you back.' Priest said, and pressed the studs to break the connections. He glanced at Silk. 'Are you thinking the same thing as myself?'

'Great minds . . . he may be blackmailing Marie.'

'Right. We see him this morning. I'm against anyone knowing she's here.'

'So am I. Her former East German and Russian friends must have seen us leave and had their friends watch us arrive. But I'm sure we shook off any one who tried to follow us from Heath Row.'

Their discussion on how to interview Denning without antagonising their dear old enemies in MI 5 was interrupted by another buzz. Priest pressed the stud again.

'Yes?'

'Sir George and Mr. Monkman are here, sir.'

'Send them in,' Priest said. He pressed the stud and stood up. 'We'll keep this to ourselves for awhile. Polish up your smile, Dorian.'

Silk gleamed wanly. 'Next time send me somewhere interesting, yes?' he pleaded. 'No city. I can't bear 'em. They give me the flaming habdabs.'

'A desert,' Priest promised soothingly. 'We'll keep this

short. Ah, come in, Sir George, Julian.'

Sir George Oxinden was a short compact man verging on tubbiness. His blue eyes sparkled like indoor fireworks. He had the silver-grey hair and white moustache which impressible impresarios regarded as symbolic of both aristocracy, and diplomacy. Instead he had started as an advertising agent and joined Intelligence during the last war. His pale grey suit, silver cravat, and grey suede shoes, were his year-long attire.

Julian Monkman was a big heavy man in his late thirties who radiated an atmosphere of rugger and beer and Sunday golf courses. He looked offensively healthy. A careless grey flannel suit looked as if the cat had her kittens in it. Thick black hair rioted over his head. Warm brown eyes looked out from his chubby face. He had come from university and Whitehall.

Their discussion over aspects of the Kremlin's treatment of British tourists in Russian gaols did not take long. Oxinden was furious.

'I don't care a damn what the blasted politicians say,' he declared irritably. 'It's monstrous. Its whole logic is warped. It makes a mockery of their pretence to want better relations. What do you think, Silk? You know these people.'

'May I misquote Clauswitz? I think the Kremlin regards peace as a continuation of war by other means. It's not going to call off its belief of shoving the entire world into acceptance of communism just when it's helped along by humanitarian governments which it regards as weak.'

Monkman nodded. 'The Kremlin will seize every advantage,' he said. His deep gravelly voice had the sonorous quality of a stage bishop.

'Exactly!' Oxinden exclaimed furiously. 'And who can outlast the Russians? Countries close to her lack the time and means to defend themselves unless they receive worthwhile guarantees of support from more powerful countries. It's like living in a new Ice Age with people in authority wambling on "We must do something about it" and doing bugger all while the ice spreads farther and farther and these bastards debate this or call for that and perjure their brains by swearing everything is just bloody fine now and getting better all the time. A load of manure! And by God I didn't spend six years of my youth fighting the bloody Nazis after they'd goosestepped over a third of Europe, and I do mean fight, just to let the bloody Russians goosestep over the whole of it. What'll happen to those yelling students and wildcat strikers if their little comrades take over here? Do they really think anyone will pay the slightest bloody attention to them if we get the comrades squatting on their arses in Whitehall?'

He was a very angry man.

Silk seldom felt an urge to kiss anyone shaped like himself. He was not a professional footballer or Judas or a welcoming Com dictator. But on this early Monday morning he had to restrain an unsexual desire to do homage to plain speaking.

Monkman and he smiled at each other. Silent laughter caused the big man to quiver like a blancmange trying to do itself a mischief.

'Will you support me?' Oxinden asked brusquely. 'Monkman and the others have already approved a note I've drafted to the Foreign Secretary.'

'I will,' Priest assured him.

Oxinden turned to Silk. 'How about you?' he demanded.

'My name means nothing here. I doubt if the F.S. ever heard of me.'

'Hurt?'

'Wounded, deeply wounded.'

'You'll live,' Oxinden said. 'I expect you miss the Middle East. It gets a hold on some. Too many bloody flies for my liking. And those camels. Disgusting!' A reminiscent gleam brightened his eyes until they looked about to give off blue sparks. 'Remind me some time to tell you about a camel which kept me awake down the

Nile. Or is it up?'

Silk blinked and shook his head. 'My sense of direction is terrible.' he admitted.

Priest cleared his throat. 'You'll have to excuse us,' he said. 'We are on our way to the new offices to hunt up some data.'

As the door closed on the other men he pressed the voice stud. 'A car rightaway.' he ordered.

'There have been developments, sir.'

'Yes?'

'We have Denning. He's waiting for you to interview him. More importantly, a man posing as a window-cleaner got into the flat and tried to shoot the German woman while she was asleep. Two of our men foiled him. He shot one, a leg injury, and got away down the fire-escape. Our other men caught him on the ground. They're holding him in an empty flat.'

'What about the woman?'

'She slept through it. One of our men is still guarding her.'

Priest glanced at Silk. 'We're on our way,' he said.

They scarcely spoke while they were driven into the demented hazards of London traffic. Only a few years ago whole neighbourhoods of suburban districts along their route, which escaped damage by bombs and doodlebugs and rockets during World War Two, had the shabby charm peculiar to terraced three-storeyed Victorian houses. Each had shown gleaming brasswork on glossy white or green double doors under a shining fan-light and most had flowers behind their ground-floor windows. No local industry had polluted the local air. Every side-street which had a few shops was a village with its separate identity. Originally these houses were homes for an expanding middle-class determined to raise large families. During and after the war they had been rented by bombed-out importers and solicitors and dentists who needed a working site for their activities.

Now they were rooming houses. Behind dingy front doors whose paintwork was flaking and cobwebbed fanlights decorated with dead flies were gloomy hallways with ancient strips of linoleum along the centre of bare and grimy boards and drab walls partly illuminated by an electric light-bulb encrusted with roasted flies. They smelled of people and last week's cooking and cats. In every house you heard the twentyfour-hour nervous throb of the city and its by-products, a cacophony of radios and television and family rows.

When Silk last wandered around here, in search of a background for a play, the whole atmosphere made him feel antique and depressed and aware of dingy death around a corner. Most people he had passed looked blank or worried and teenagers seemed to be the prey of endless agitation. And around one corner he had come upon a Russian television crew lovingly filming these seedy regions, presumably for a documentary to persuade viewers in the USSR that this was representative of every British working-class district.

At that time he had known the region well. He and his then wife had lived in a block of flats in an adjoining district. His then wife had been a night-club chanteuse. She had not passed as 'wife' for long; he had never understood why the clergy in its innocence assumed that a licence established a permanent condition of spirit able to withstand pressures and changes. A couple of years ago he read somewhere that she was a linnet in Los Angeles.

Priest's voice interrupted his thoughts.

'I think it better to change my mind on a couple of points.'

'Why not? One is you've decided to bring in MI 5 rather than have a row.'

'Our fashionable city word for it is confrontation. It will avoid a harassment.'

'Please, repeat the last word . . . oh, is that the fashionable pronunciation? They don't half muck about nowadays. How unimpressive.'

Priest laughed. 'Our fashionable city word for impressive or anything similar is dramatic.' he said. 'If you listen to the radio news bulletins you'll hear them chucking 'dramatic' and 'crisis' about like stale liquorice all-sorts. Both words have become meaningless . . . yes, unless we bring in Five now they'll scream to someone at the F.O. who'll run to the P.M. Secondly, I'll drop you in order you can get back to your girl friend and I'll interview Denning alone. I want her watched.'

'Right.'

'You'll have to take her somewhere else while we decide what to do. They're bound to try to get to her again.'

'I don't understand how they found the flat. I'd swear I shook them off during the drive from the airport.'

'They may have known about it before you brought her.'

'True.'

'I'll drop you so that you can get a bus and walk there. If anyone follows you play it cool. They may lead us to Jeremy.'

'Uh-huh.'

'Stay with her every moment.'

'You really don't know what you're asking,' Silk told him. 'Why not give her to the police?'

'Think.'

' . . . Jeremy will get to know?'

'He may. Someone in Berlin told him she came here with you. At any rate, it seems like it. To the best of our knowledge, she isn't an East German subject so their diplomatic people can't ask to see her. They have to use other methods to silence her.'

After a pause Silk said: 'If I was Jeremy I might imagine she would know my identity. On the other hand, Jeremy may know that she knows who he is. In either case, he could feel himself in a very dicey position.'

Priest nodded gently. 'Yes,' he agreed, 'and it's my guess he knows you. Therefore he will assume you brought her here to tell all.'

Silk smiled sourly. 'It would help you if someone tried to kill me so our people could catch him,' he said.

'Your Monday morning brain has improved,' Priest assured him complacently. 'Right. After I've seen Denning I'll come to St. Martin's Court, next door to your block, to find out what has happened and arrange where you shall take her. I'll give you a call about two.' He thought for a moment, and added: 'I'll drive myself after I've dropped you. Avery can go along as your bodyguard. I don't want you too exposed here.'

'Oh, ta, very much, yes, any place else but not here.'

'Correct.' Priest said, and switched on the gadget to talk to their driver.

Silk got off the bus into a late morning swarm of women harassed by children. Only a few men were about on their feet; most of them hid inside cars. Other cars snoozed unpeacefully nose to tail along the curbs giving off their oily stench. In the past decade every London street had become a dormitory for cars, a geriatric dormitory if stories of there inbuilt obsolescence were true. They and an armoured security corps truck outside a bank provided proof that a certain charm had gone out of London life.

At a battery of traffic lights he waited until a change of colour gained sullen compliance from road-users. Then he and other unfashionable people on their feet crossed over. Then he paused again to cross at right angles, went on a short distance, and turned left down another drowsy sunlit road lined by cars but with horse-chestnut trees burdened by waxy pink and white candles to relieve the optical monotony. Through open gateways he saw gravel drives and white-painted family mansions snug amid well-shaven lawns and flower-beds full of geraniums or white roses, here and there a maiden-auntly hydrangea, trees in full leaf. All this area was doomed. He knew the local council was waiting for residents to leave or die off and then fling up a vast estate of high-rise blocks.

At present everything was placid and friendly. Nothing disturbed the peacefulness except three or four airplanes hovering around for permission to land at Heathrow.

When he glanced round as if uncertain of his whereabouts he saw nothing sinister. A milk roundsman stacked cartons of yoghurt into his wire basket. An inquisitive taxi peered into each gateway like a drunk uncertain of his way home. Both of the carless housewives laden with larder replenishments had not bothered about any man for the last ten years. Some paces farther back was the tall figure of Avery, anonymous, a man inside a dark city suit with pencil-thin trousers and a bowler hat tilted back from his forehead. Passing him at a rate of knots was a tall striding teenage girl with sleek blonde hair descending from a central parting to her breasts and from the other end a fine pair of nylon adverts to ten inches above her knees: between the two was a long-sleeved mustard-yellow dress and a red handbag suspended on a broad strap over her left shoulder. Both of the housewives gazed blankly at her and forgot about her. An ice-cream van tinkled its unmusical bells.

As he went on he saw only trees and gateways, speeding cars and a dozen or so people going along their paths of purpose, and in the distance a vision of the sunlit upper storeys of modern low-rise blocks of flats rising above trees where the old houses ended.

He was defeated by the location. Security wagons for banknotes and bullion or not, it was too suburban-cosy to hint at menaces of the sort to which he reacted instinctively. He understood the dangers of foreign locations. This scene, with its unlovely ice-cream van chimes and distant peals of laughter from unseen children, leant too gently on his mind. Nothing would ever qualify him for work in MI 5.

As the long-legged girl passed him she fumbled at a packet of cigarettes taken from her handbag and then turned to face him, tapping a cigarette on a blood-red thumb-nail. 'Have you a light, please?' she asked.

While he snapped on the lighter he had on him to serve others, he thought it a pity she wasn't just legs. She was a few years older than he had estimated. Her legs led to schoolboy-narrow hips and a flat waistless body; she had shown good sense to cover arms which were probably thin pallid tubes of unshaped flesh. Her long hollow-cheeked face was unimproved by miniature blue thunderclouds smeared above hazel eyes and lilac lipstick which argued with her greyish skin. He realized the bright sheen of her blonde hair came from a bottle and her bony hands trembled uncontrollably. At the same instant his ears told the inquisitive taxi was picking up speed. He reacted intuitively.

Before the girl could say anything he snapped off the lighter and picked up her bundle of matchsticks weight and ran forward. Although the cigarette fell from her lips she neither screamed nor spoke, her head drooping on his left shoulder in the manner of a weary child. Through each fragmented second he was aware of the deep purr of the accelerating taxi rising above the gay chimes from the ice-cream wagon. Fourteen strides took him and his bundle to the nearest tree. As he reached it someone inside the taxi started to fire. A gnat-storm of bullets flew around them as he tripped the girl and sprawled down on her as she fell wearily on her back. Things from her bag spilled over the pavement. He heard a woman scream like a skidding taxi.

6

Gradually the sound of the taxi receded towards the distant blocks of flats. He stayed down. Not too long ago a bunch of Com Arabs had nearly caught him unprepared by sending an armed party in a second car immediately the first had disappeared.

No purposeful movement came from beneath him. She merely trembled. A sour breath came from her open mouth. His first movement brought her eyes towards him. They were dull as old dustbins, their pupils unable to focus. Their vacancy was familiar. As Avery halted breathlessly above them, he got to his knees and undid her sleeves and yanked them up. Inside each elbow was a nest of needle punctures. She looked at him with eyes older than the Sphinx, drained of every ordinary emotion. He had met great-grandmothers a damn sight younger of heart and fitter of body and mind.

'Why?' he asked curtly.

'They promised me a fix if I stopped you, man.'

She pronounced they as 'thee' and you as 'yew'.

'How were you to get it?'

'Round the next corner. They'll send someone to give it to me like. Y' got a fix for me? I been three days without one, y' know, man. I'll come home with y' if y' give me one.'

A cough brought blood from her mouth. It was the first indication that she had been wounded. Almost immediately he saw blood oozing across the dusty pavement from her left side. An attempt to say something ended as she winced painfully. As she tried to sit up his hand kept her down.

'Stay there,' he told her, and spoke over his shoulder to Avery. 'Did you get its number?'

'Yes, sir.'

'Tell those women to get help. This girl needs attention.'

As if they were a duet the women said: 'It's nothing to do with us' and 'We don't want to get involved'. They trudged on. So did a man in a business suit carrying a brief-case. So did a blue car which had halted for its occupants, another white-collared man and a woman in a magenta chiffon scarf and dark sun-glasses, to see excitement.

'Stop a car,' Silk snarled angrily.

'They go straight on.'

'Run to one of the houses and call an ambulance and get the police,' Silk said and took off his jacket to cover the shivering girl. 'Don't move, honey. Stay where you are.'

'I got stitch in my side, man, it's painful, man. Give me a fag.'

She took a deep breath while she spoke and it brought a run of blood from her mouth. He heard shocked whispers between people gathering behind him; he was shocked too but he had work to do.

'We'd better wait, honey,' he said. 'What's your name?'

'Maureen Oakroyd,'

'Where is your real home?'

'One five two Greenhalgh Crescent, Liverpool.'

'Where do you you live here?'

She gave a choked giggle which brought another gush of blood. 'A girl can usually get some feller to share his pad like y' know till she gets her own,' she said, and shut her eyes abruptly. Her breathing was becoming laboured.

He felt helpless, sure she was bleeding to death.

'It shouldn't be allowed!' exclaimed an incensed female voice behind him.

He turned on his knees. Well-shod feet led to decorated brown matador trousers stretched on well-fleshed thighs and buttocks and a bronze silk blouse which covered an ample bosom. Above them was a strong neck and a plump fortyish well-made-up face. Everything about her appearance fitted the socially conscious voice, imitation Girton. He had seen kindlier expressions on a female face. Alongside her, drawn into the curb, was a newish car, door wide open, engine still running. There were about a dozen other people.

'Will you help me get this girl to a hospital in your car?' he asked.

'I wouldn't let such a creature into my car,' the woman said in an accusative voice. 'I saw what happened. She's a dope addict. And I don't know who you are. Girls like her shouldn't be allowed!'

He stared up at her indignant, carefully tended face, a mask of indulgent good living. Suddenly he lost patience.

'Who the hell allowed them to come into existence, you pious idiot?' he rasped at her. 'Clear off, you make me sick. Clear off, the lot of you.'

After several 'How dare you?' exclamations, the stupid bitch gave up. She got back into her car and drove off at high speed.

When Avery came back some minutes later he was still squatting on his heels. Several people and cars had stopped, then gone on. He looked up at Avery, narrowing his eyes against the strong sunlight.

'They're coming, sir,' the man told him as he crouched down.

'Good.'

'She seems quieter.'

'Dead people usually are.'

Avery hissed through his teeth.

'How?'

'One in her left lung and one somewhere high up on the spine.'

A car braked violently to a halt alongside. A small balding man got out and joined them.

'I'm a doctor,' he said crisply. 'What's wrong?'

Priest strode into the flat Silk used in his role of Philip Foot. One of Silk's bodyguards sat huddled on a chair staring at his hands. He looked like a man who had been caught trying to enter a nunnery at night. Silk got to his feet.

'Sorry to interrupt your plan,' he said, and tried to keep anger out of his voice. 'Good of you to come immediately.'

'Better we should discuss it rightaway. When did she vanish?'

'It must have happened about the time we left your office.'

'What happened?'

'From what I can tell,' Silk answered in a dangerous tone, 'this fool went to a celebration party last night and drank too much. It upset his stomach. Being a strong rugged independent type, the sort which never gives up for fear of losing face, he didn't tell anyone he wasn't feeling too good. Twice he left the flat and went to a rest-room along the corridor. He was sure she was asleep each time he left. When he got back the second time she was gone.'

Priest looked at the man. 'Is that correct?' he asked. His voice made Silk's sound like a cooing dove.

'. . .sir.'

'Why the hell didn't you tell someone or report sick?'

Their assistant's homely features registered distinct anxiety. Nothing singled him out from millions of men who rode home in tubes or hire-purchase cars. Even his wife probably forgot what he looked like directly he left home. Evidently this facelessness was his only qualification for their work.

'I was never afflicted by the necessity on duty before, sir,' he answered in a pained tone. 'Normally my capacity to withstand the effects of some convivial drinking has never occasioned me concern.' He sounded bewildered and miffed, distinctly miffed. 'This gentleman,' he added, ignoring Silk, 'has expressed himself to me in what I can only describe as language he would not employ if he knew I belonged to a trade union.'

'Too bad,' Priest said, 'too bad.' Then his voice sharpened. 'So you'd better get out before I tell you what I think of a man who comes on duty without informing anyone of his condition. Out.' Directly the door shut he went on: 'Have you any idea where she might have gone?'

Silk sat down on an easy chair. 'None,' he replied shortly.

'No note?'

'No.'

Priest played church with his fingers. His face gave no

clue to his thoughts. After some minutes he fished out a handkerchief to wipe under his chin. 'Those pills you gave her must have been below strength,' he commented. 'I'll have the whole consignment destroyed.'

'Thanks for the confidence. I did give her the correct dose.'

'You don't have to reassure me.'

Priest nodded. 'Tell me about the girl and what happened,' he said. 'I imagine our people are trying to check on her.'

'I got them onto it immediately. They may have no leads here. I searched her bag without finding a London address or letter written to her here. She had only a few shillings. She may have been a squatter.'

'We'll search junkie discothéques and cafes for news. What happened?'

Promptly at two-thirty Silk strode into the flat in St. Martin's Court. Priest looked up from a chair facing the windows. His eyes held a question.

'Nothing yet,' Silk told him. 'How about Denning?'

'Affable and truculent.'

'He talked.'

'Yes. He says she paid him a thousand pounds in order to get a British passport. He swears they parted a month after the wedding. I gather he has no wish to see her again. Apparently her attitude to some things offended his modesty. He says his money comes from his being one of a syndicate of four which won nearly two hundred thousand pounds on a football pool. He and his present "wife" are unmarried because she is married to a Roman Catholic who refuses to divorce her. I think he is telling the truth, but we're checking. He had a ring of truth about him.'

'How did he meet his previous wife?'

'They were staying at a Kensington hotel and met in its bar. He says she was lonely and oversexed and unpopular. I gather she talked a lot about having a serious heart condition. She paid him the thousand because he was reluctant to marry a foreigner.'

'That's a new excuse.'

'Did they tell you the man who tried to shoot Marie managed to get away while they were taking him to the police station for interview?'

'They told me. No comment.'

When the telephone interrupted the ten-to-nine evening telenews Silk picked up the receiver and listened briefly and said: 'Not yet.'

He was halfway through a breakfast of eggs and bacon, honey and toast and coffee, when there was a ring at the front door. A solitary envelope awaited him on the mat. Its luxuriant female handwriting was familiar. Its King's Cross postmark meant nothing.

He opened it and drew out the letter inside which began:

'Philip, my darling love, for that is what you are; are you mine, really mine? I want you to be, as wholly and completely as I am yours. Beloved, I wrote you a little note to explain why I must leave you for a few days and in my hurry I slipped it into my handbag. I am such a silly woman, my darling, I need you to keep me in order. Now I cannot find your telephone number because the directories here are out of date and have pages missing. So I have to write and tell you that soon after you left me alone I called an old friend of mine and heard she is very ill in Edinburgh so I am going to Scotland to see her.

Süsser, I will be back directly I can because I want to be only with you. I have never felt like this before. Do not be jealous or afraid I shall look at another man. When I feel close to anyone as I do to you there is no one else I can see, they are shadows passing me in the street. I will come back to you, *mein Liebhaber, mein Leibster.* It will only be for a few days and already I am mad with longing to feel you against me and have your hands and lips upon me as I did on our first glorious night, already I am thinking of small things I hope will please you. . .'

He took a breath and felt behind his ears. They were remarkably dry; they had been for years. He buttered another slice of toast and read on. She must have been sitting inside a refrigerator to need to stir up such heat.

When he finished breakfast he went back into the bathroom and washed his hands carefully.

He went back into the bedroom and found a tie some degrees more cheerful than his mood and knotted it carefully under his collar. It was clear that Marie did not intend to return of her own free will but he supposed he should raise one small cheer that she imagined him to be a fool; it might come in handy later on. Unless he was vastly mistaken she intended to assume her other identity here until she felt safe and then she might do anything or go anywhere. It seemed unlikely she would use her passport as Denning's wife at this stage in an attempt to leave the country.

He shrugged into his jacket and went for an athletic prowl round the flat whistling softly. First and foremost, he had to stay here for a few days in case some incident caused her to panic and come to him for help. Secondly, it became more clear with every hour that she must know where to get money and assume another identity. A widow? No, he doubted it in her case because she was still sufficiently young to need social companionship if no more. A businesswoman? More likely. Everyone treated the peccadillos of lone businesswomen indulgently. Probably one who travelled extensively, which would account for her long absences.

He padded into the kitchen to brew a jug of fresh coffee while he washed up the breakfast things.

While they were having lunch the following Monday Priest said: 'I think we can assume she does not intend to return to your loving arms.'

Silk raised his brows and went on enjoying his cold

turkey and ham and the best salad he had met for years.

'It's a pity this happened,' Priest commented. 'You know why. We have to assume Jeremy knows your identity. He would arrange for you to be picked up and exchanged for her. You would be trapped and questioned by their usual methods. You'd be far from home, without a gun, friendless, unable to trot round to the Embassy for help.'

Silk sampled his chablis. It was a good vintage and the label was genuine. 'Grim,' he agreed as he put down his glass. 'Theories often are. Yes?'

'You know we have to assume the worse.'

'What happens about the information you wanted? If my memory is not too fogged by these tumultuous events it involves Russian naval plans to dominate the Med and material on the fight by intellectuals. You remember you finally told they were led by this Professor Konuzin.'

'We'll let it alone for awhile.'

'Ah ? And me? Do I wait around for someone to take a pot-shot at me and kill some poor kid who doesn't know anything about the world outside of pushers and pop, porno and pot? Has there been any lead from the abandoned taxi? What about the man who tried to kill her? Has he been caught?'

'Not yet. We'll find you something to do.'

Silk finished his wine. He replaced the glass. 'I feel involved in this thing,' he commented. 'It shouldn't be let alone. In fact, I expect you already intend to send someone else. They will be in exactly the same spot as myself because we have to assume Jeremy is another Philby. I know Moscow. Maybe this other individual does too, but so do I. And Primakov told you my Russian is not too dusty, just gritty in the grammer, its declensions.' He scratched an itch on his nose. 'I've a better idea. You tell everyone, every single individual concerned, you think it should be left alone. Tell them I've gone to report on guerrillas in Jordan or what's happening in Iran or to write Nassah's memoirs. Let me go.'

'Dicey.'

'So help me, it's getting dicey just to be an ordinary individual in this country. Besides, I'm involved. I've been far more involved since Czechoslovakia was invaded. I'm not a politician with a convenient memory and a long spoon for supping with the devil. Moreover, I can't stay here. With a general election and international football coming upon us, I'd be bored to death. Life is too short for such dullery.'

Priest shook his head regretfully. 'Sorry, no,' he decided. 'You tempt me, but no. It would be too great a risk.'

7

As Silk strode briskly up the rise to pass the architecturally indigestible clot of St. Basil's Cathedral, one of those garish onion-domed lollipop structures which his Gothic-attuned eye always found a bit much, he saw that Red Square was already busy.

He was smiling. He was worried. Although Strelnikov was not due to contact him until tomorrow, Konuzin had already failed to appear on three of the alternate dates arranged for their first meeting. If Konuzin did not keep their appointment this evening it could only mean that something had indeed gone wrong and the KGB had already acted on information supplied by Jeremy through Marie. It brought him up-tight against danger.

He tried to push the nasty little niggle out of his mind to ensure he kept a relaxed expression on his handsome face.

Although the hour was early the usual queue of adherents plus foreign package-deal tourists had started to form ahead on his left among spruce trees in front of the squat red and black stone Lenin Mausoleum. If the black and dull grey suits of the men and bright print dresses of the women were a true guide the vast majority of them were provincial Heroes of Labour whose increased productivity over several years had earned them a brief sightseeing glimpse of the capital of their empire and a room at one of the hotels not listed to attract foreign visitors. To them the mausoleum, their national shrine, more unifying than the red brick-walled Kremlin behind it, was a source of inspiration. Their presence here amounted to a religious pilgrimage.

On previous visits to Moscow he had seen ageing men and women weep as they went slowly past the crystal sarcophagus containing the embalmed corpse of Lenin with its tinted cheeks and carefully dyed hair. He had once heard a rumour that the body was the fourth substituted for the dead Bolshevik but doubted it.

Irrespective of politics, Silk always thought embalmed bodies more than slightly gruesome, a combination of primitive nature and advertising. But authentic or not they did have an emotional effect on some people. He supposed some people wept here because of the atmosphere of the tomb. Others probably wept because the *shiroky* nature, the 'broad' temperament, of Russians needed to express positive emotions. He suspected many wept because they had seen the bright dream of their youth kicked to death by leaders who had won power struggles since Lenin died, their wartime sacrifices ignored, and knew the party bosses had conned them. But every day except during the hardest winter spells they lined up for this visit to the Holy Tomb to see their religion's Divine Relics, guided past the deified bier by guardians of the sepulchre. Many of those who crept forward on their journey of homage were men and women whose names headed the *Doska Pochota,* Honours Board of best workers, at their factories. This early huddle meant they had a full day of sight-seeing ahead of them.

Across the square other groups were already standing outside the windows of GUM, the State Department Store. Most people there were drably attired and middleaged, solidly built as if to withstand the rigours of Moscow's long and penalising winters. Such women were often seen clearing snow or shoving a clattery pneumatic drill into the road somewhere. They were clearly window-shopping; they had neither the income nor the figures for the mass-produced goods which attracted their curiosity. GUM was still the largest *suq* in this part of the world, unquestionably an Oriental bazaar despite its pretentious Victorian facade. Every time he entered it he could smell camels. Along its arcades were small shops similar to those in *suqs* he had visited from Casablanca to Kabul. He always expected to find older women there wearing a *yashmaq* or shrouded in an *aba*.

Ahead of him a quartette of Red Army officers walked past the Museum of History towards Manege Square. They were desk wallahs. Each carried a brief-case, delicately, as if it contained lunch sandwiches and a fragile pastry.

He saw that the queue outside Lenin's Tomb contained a sprinkling of colonial subjects. Among Russian faces, round and pale and flattish with high malar bones above thick cheeks and wide-lipped mouths, were others with more richly toned skin and black eyes and other facial characteristics of people from the colonial territories heaped above Afghanistan and stretching east across central Asia. There were several widely beaming young Africans and a trio of enigmatic Indians. Behind two blue-turbaned Sikhs was a white-haired couple whose clothes had a South American appearance.

He slowed down and looked around as if unfamiliar with this heart of the empire, the core of an ever-widening spill of Russian red on the map.

He went on again and then halted to gaze at the bridal-cake top of Nikolskaya Tower under its green steeple and red star. Then he heeled round again to look at the sunlit Spasskaya Tower, through whose gateway Czars and their retinues had entered the Kremlin.

At once a prickle of tension went up his spine.

Poised on the square, midway between the entrance to Spasskaya Tower and the Lobnoye Mesto, Place of Execution, in front of St. Basil's, and looking for all the world like a large leprechaun caught without a bush to hide behind, was his shadow. But he was no leprechaun in size. By Russian standards he was huge, all of five feet eight and solid as one of those tractor-drivers or blue-shirted factory foremen whose muscle-bound postures were the ideal of Soviet 'realistic' art. Even at this distance he looked as if his Mama had raised him on granite chips for breakfast cereals to achieve the jaw illuminated by sunlight. He had sandy hair cut Prussian style, a real skin-head. He would have made a lovely cuddly plaything for those former Olympic belles, the lissom and feminine Press sisters.

Silk had seen him on previous days. He had also seen the other three. One, the most noticeable, was a small man who crept around like a drunken spider. His two colleagues were nondescript men whose wives would have to be introduced to them again in a crowd of two others. They were ideal security men. There were certain to be others. Since Russian tanks crushed Czechoslovakia Soviet security men had multiplied like rabbits.

Ostensibly, they were the usual loose end shadows who attached themselves to any beyond-the-curtain foreigner who took a walk without an official guide. He had seen them pin themselves onto his own innocent colleagues at the exhibition, Nicholas Hennessy and David Keene, typical of young British business representatives, devoted to their cars and golf and do-it-yourself kits and wives, and the last member of the team, Martha Conroy. She had known she was being followed. She told him about it. On the fringe of early middle age she was unmarried. She was tall and slim and had an atmosphere of ravaged good looks, heightened by her restlessness and unquiet brown eyes. She had pale brown hair and a preference for pale brown knitted gowns. Directly any of them left the hotel a shadow pinned itself onto them. Whether they were just ordinary shadows he had no means of deciding.

He turned slowly on his heels and strolled down the incline past the Historical Museum and on across Revolution Square and past the Moskva Hotel. Then he turned right on Karl Marx Prospekt and turned into Sverdlov Square with the huge tree-flanked statue of Marx, facing the Bolshoi Theatre, ahead on his right.

When he paused on the corner as if uncertain whether to go and admire the flower-beds and clumps of trees in front of the Bolshoi, he saw that his bulky Leprechaun was there not too far behind him. He turned right again, skirting the square, and headed towards the Metro station and Red Square.

Another prickle of tension eddied up his spine. Something could have gone wrong. Easily enough. At the drop of a syllable he could be arrested on any of a dozen charges.

He walked through a party of sailors sightseeing like himself. Away from their voices he acknowledged that up to now no one had given an indication of knowing his identity. To this precise moment the ploys had been the familiar Russian gambits. At an informal party for representatives at the exhibition a Russian official, Vladimir Maslov, had introduced him to a man named Anatoli Gromov who had tried to persuade him to go on to a private drinking party. When that failed he found himself talking to a big handsome tallow-blonde reputedly named Nina Alexandrova, fashioned to give comfort and to create a feeling of conquest in any male breast, and then to Valya Volkova, an attractive brunette of lesser but equally delightful dimensions and introduced as a widow, and clearly there to show gratitude for sympathy. After the girls wandered off to less disinterested individuals Gromov had introduced him to a willowy type named Yuri Pekelis, but Silk was a lifelong heterosexual despite all. This was the normal routine window display to win friends for Russia among visiting businessmen and politicians who could become blackmailed into being weak little men.

Abruptly a small plump man came nimbly towards him with a careful stare of light grey eyes. As abruptly a smile spread over the broad Russian face as if its owner recognized him. It hovered there like a butterfly on a stone and probably fluttered off as Silk walked past without any sign of recognition.

Some paces farther on Silk drew a long slow breath. It contained a cautious measure of relief. Why should they waste effort on offering him standard inducements to witlessness if they already knew his identity? Within one second his brief illusion of confidence died the death. They might have decided to give him the routine treatment to lull him into a false belief of security in order to find out if he would lead them to Konuzin and Strelnikov.

He felt coldness in his nostrils as he walked on among scores of Russians and turned left round the Lenin Museum into Red Square. You could never tell what devious scheme the Asiatic mind of Russian officialdom might devize.

His lips had gone dry. He tried to cheer himself up with a realization that hundreds of British agents had run far greater risks, particularly the men and women of SOE who had gone into Nazi-held Europe during World War Two. Their unsung service had a long tradition of audacity in the service of their country during bad and good times from the days of Francis Walsingham, spymaster of Elizabeth I. And his own section, the old firm of MI 6, was now fighting both against the positive cold war tactics of Moscow, pursuing its imperialist ends by every available means from arms sales to fomenting wildcat strikes around the world, and the apathetic indolence of parish-pump politicians. He thought the game worth the candle.

He strode on, sweating it out in his waking brain, the way agents do while they endure unexplained delays in countries run by hostile governments.

After he had passed GUM on his return he paused to look across Red Square at the tomb of Lenin. A party of brown-uniformed soldiers goose-stepped like automatons to the shrine-tomb of the first communist czar to take over guard duty. According to Professor Konuzin the new regime of communism had merely replaced the old czarism with a greater and more rigid authoritarianism. Konuzin's friends included intellectuals who had gone to gaol and labour-camps for criticizing the present form of administration, men like Daniel and Sinyavsky, others who had managed to escape, people like Svetlana Alliluyeva and Kuznetsov and Vladimirov, and others here over whom hung the perpetual threat of death or imprisonment unless they conformed, Solzhenitsyn and Yevtushenko. Boris Pasternak had been his friend since youth. These men had noted how writers in Brezhnev's empire were denied the freedom given to writers in Czarist times, the Doestoevskys, Gogols, Turgenevs, Tolstoys, and others. That was not surprising. All communists and socialists in power were frightened of writers.

He glanced at the clock in the Spasskaya Tower and walked on at a slower pace. On balance it was better for him to be here than the other men immediately available. They had emotional ties at home which could cripple their resolves. 'It had to be me, wonderful me,' his mind hummed, abusing the old song.

Momentarily he paused to look at the onion-domes of St. Basil's. No, he did not like them. With their blue-and-white diagonal stripes, yellow criss-crossed with green, vari-studded geometric confusion, curling blue and gold strips, they reminded him of ornate turbans. Then he strode on again followed by his shadows.

When he turned into the hotel he caught sight of Leprechaun still following him. He drew a breath of relief that no one had contacted him during his walk.

He was mistaken.

Up in his room on the eighth floor he searched his pockets for a handkerchief and in the right-hand pocket of his jacket his fingers touched paper. He drew out a five-inch square of inferior typing copy paper. Mindful that a gimlet eye might be watching him through the possibly false mirror or some other spy hole, he studied it as if it were a note he had written to remind himself of something. On it someone had written a pencilled message in English and weird capital letters.

As he read it he realized that if all else failed and he lived long enough to get out of Russia alive someone could hire him as an instant ice-manufacturing machine. One chunk of it had come out of the nowhere into the here of his stomach and frozen it, and ice drops tinkled like pebbles down his arteries.

He read it again: 'Dorian—I will see you today. Brig has been detained. News will be given shortly. Do what I say. We are in trouble.'

He had read more cheerful missives. Someone knew that Konuzin was 'Brigand'. Someone knew him for himself. He hissed gently between his teeth. Strangely enough when he glanced round the room had not been lit on all sides with red lights.

A heavy rapping on the door did not improve his general condition.

'Who is it?' he called cheerfully.

'David, old man,' a hearty voice shouted. 'We're leaving. You ready?'

'Just a tick, old son.'

He could not risk the luxury of hesitation. Someone might have him under surveillance. Humming an off-key non-tune he got out his wallet and put the note in it. It was impossible to swallow it; the paper might be poisoned. He would have to get rid of it in the lavatory as they left. He put the wallet back into his pocket.

Still humming he opened the door and smiled brightly at Keene's pointed dark face. 'Come in, old son,' he said. 'I've only got to brush my hair. Leave the door open. Do you suffer from dandruff?'

'Not yet, but, God, my head,' Keene complained as he entered. 'It must have been that vodka last night. It hit me as I got out of bed. I need a round of golf to sharpen the old wits. Guess what, old man.'

'Too early for guesses, old boy.'

'A man chased Martha over Moskvoretsky Bridge. It made her day.'

'It'll give her an appetite.'

'Not for food.'

'Martha's human.'

'You watch out. She has an eye on you.'

'I'm promised,' Silk said.

He could feel the note burning through his wallet like dry ice.

8

When Silk went for lunch he was as edgy as an Olympic sprinter poised too long on fingertips and blocks waiting for the crack of the starting gun to send him hurtling up the track.

Nobody had approached him. On several occasions he had half-imagined he caught sight of a man in the crowd who resembled Strelnikov and once he thought he saw Konuzin. Each time it proved to be a false alarm. No strangers had sought his attention by giving recognition signals.

Non-developments were only part of his problems. Quite a large number of people hung around the stand for a long time. If any were KGB agents hoping to panic him into self-betrayal they failed. Outwardly he was confident.

Nevertheless, under the smile sewn on his face like an extra skin his nerves had pumped so much adrenalin into his system that he could have set up in business as a manufacturer. They also revived his latent claustrophobia. His perch on the stand, shut in by Soviet eyes, felt like the innermost of a nest of Chinese boxes. It was encased by other stands inside the large pavilion, full of deafening tangled echoes of voices and footsteps, itself surrounded by the wooded spread of Sokolniki Park. And around the park itself spread the expanding human zoo of Moscow itself. And around Moscow was Holy Russia, the eternal gaol for its native-born critics.

At moments he had a nostalgic longing to be back in Inner Mongolia surrounded by Chinese troops and wondering how the hell to get out of it. He should have had the sense to know a soft job when he had one.

Fortunately they were too busy for him to brood on his claustrophobia. That was lucky. He preferred being entombed in a bat cave with a dying torch to being mewed up in a city. Unfortunately their visitors at the stand were all government officials. That was understandable in a country which regarded private enterprise as the original sin. They came in groups, grimly affable men and wholesome women, every one of them prepared to report on each other to the authorities. They brought interpreters which saved him from having to go into a bit of theatrical business with a phrase-book. Their questions were well-informed, concerned solely with the range of programming for each computer, modifications and evolved systems used in recent years, and the degree of variability to be expected. Some might be industrial spies. Their questions were too acute to come from ordinary officials. And undoubtedly the interpreters were spies. He knew it. As the morning had worn on, he noted that, as on the previous two days, some questions and additional points added in Russian by the interpreters when they translated replies given by himself and other members of the team showed a far higher degree of scientific knowledgeability than an interpreter would need to possess. No wonder the Kremlin maintained such large trade missions abroad. He became cagier with every answer.

Around every stand streamed thousands of ordinary Muscovites and colonial visitors. Outwardly there was nothing unusual about them. They wandered about like millions of men and women the world over who had nothing particular to do on their rest days. They were poorly and drably dressed. Most men were content with dark trousers and old one-colour shirts, quite a quantity of them knitted, and the women had printed floral frocks. None glanced at him with meaning.

He was relieved to get out of the noisy heat into the sunlit wooded quietness of the park. Momentarily he paused, undecided whether to go to a restaurant near the main entrance or to one he had discovered yesterday beyond the library. He decided on the latter and set off along the side path. If anyone wanted to contact him they might find it easier in one of the less commotive cafes. On the other hand it might well be that no one would contact him. He could not be sure. Had the note been a trap by someone who imagined they knew him, an attempt to get him to betray himself? Had anyone seen the note passed to him, Leprechaun or another shadow? He had no positive answer to either question. If anyone really suspected him they had only to arrest him without any fuss. An enemy would know that the note must put him on his guard. But the Russian mind was very devious.

He took his time as he wandered among trees skirting a clubhouse for those who sought quietness, and then crossed a path and walked among more trees behind the library. Fortunately there were few people here. He had a good feeling of being alone to do some thinking about his problems.

'Mr. Foot.'

He recognized the tight sharp voice. It belonged to Martha Conroy. While his mind cursed he repinned his convivial smile on his aching cheekbones, dragged his lips apart, and let boyish brightness light his eyes. Then he swung round athletically on his heels. It nearly did him a considerable mischief.

'Miss Conroy!' he exclaimed gladly.

As she came towards him across the shadow-dappled grass her long thin face had its habitual expression of hopeful resentment. In fact, he had never seen her without it. Every day she wore it like other women affected a particular hair-style.

Although tall she appeared taller on account of long legs visible to some four inches above her knees and a slender body whose soft contours were unconcealed by her pale brown dress. Her hazel eyes had a starved expression. They seemed to probe every crowd angrily as if searching it for someone trying to hide from her. She could have done a little to assist her appearance but opted for the public image of a highly-strung businesswoman above such frills.

He had a guilty feeling that he was condemning her too roughly because of the deplorable Marie. That one would give anyone ulcers in the mind. He relaxed his smile.

'Coming for lunch?' he asked.

'Do you mind if I come with you?' she asked tautly. 'I don't feel safe.'

That made two of them.

'I almost asked you to come,' he said. 'I think we should all get to know each other instead of being careful strangers meeting for the first time. But you were busy with Nicolas Hennessy. Forget about the man who followed you. Men do follow women. Everywhere.'

She matched her stride to his, another indication of loneliness. Somehow she managed to give herself the atmosphere of a prowling tigress, heightened by her habit of looking round from side to side as they paced through the sunlight and shadow. He saw no group of amorous Russians likely to rush.

'I shall recommend that the company send two ladies on these foreign visits,' she declared angrily.

He pulled down the eyebrow which always started to lift itself at the use of 'lady' or 'ladies'. 'You mustn't dwell on it,' he advised. 'It happens in Britain.'

'Oh, I can take care of myself in Britain.'

They managed to find an empty table in the *kafe* near

one of the lakes.

Most people at other tables were youngish married couples with a child or two. Their general attire, allowing for differences of skirt length and other trivial details, differed little from what people in European industrial towns wore in the nineteen-thirties. As it was a hot day most women were bare-legged and hatless. They wore printed cotton frocks of inferior quality or a simple white or pale blue blouse with a dark knee-length skirt, most of them home-made, and white court shoes. Their hair was unfailingly neat. Collectively and individually they were trim and attractive. Among the men those who were unmarried stood out because their shirts were usually of a darker blue. Family men favoured white shirts with long sleeves or pale blue shirts with short sleeves. Some wore a serviceable dark suit which would cost about £70 if the rouble was taken at its official exchange rate but was closer to £20, which itself was high for those whose weekly wage varied from £3.5.0 to £7.15.0 in actual purchasing power. Every man had a Saturday-before-the-war hair-clip, short back and sides. There were no hippies. No flowing manes. No Fu Manchu Voortrekker beards worn by anti-apartheid demonstrators. No Carnaby Street gear.

He would like to know what went on inside their indoctrinated minds. Glancing round while Martha Conroy and he ate *zakuskis*, the national *hors d'oeuvres*, he was pretty sure it started with being intensely patriotic Russians and to hell with everyone else. Everywhere he had gone he had been conscious of a deep patriotic spirit binding Russians together. They were conscious of being the men and women whose country ruled a vast empire and whose soldiers with their formidable hardware could crush the independence of neighbouring smaller countries with a ruthlessness greater than that of capitalist countries precisely because it claimed to have forsworn the use of military aggression.

Although none appeared to be interested in him or his

companion he had no feeling of safety. He was perched on a knife edge and would remain there till he got out of this heart of empire.

He resented small talk when many things required his urgent attention.

They had finished eating and were discussing business over fruit drinks when a soft insistent voice claimed attention.

'May I join you, Mr. Foot?'

A peppermill creak of Russian accent overlaid the English words.

Yuri Pekelis smiled down at him.

Silk was puzzled over why they persisted along this line. 'Sit down,' he invited the Russian cheerfully. 'This is a surprise. Do you know Miss Conway? We would be lost without her. Have you eaten?'

Pekelis gave Martha a smile of winsome loathing. 'I had a snack with friends,' he said, and fixed a caressive gaze on Silk. 'How are you?' He made the question sound as if Silk had barely survived some ghastly calamity.

'Fine,' Silk assured him heartily. 'Have you recovered from that wonderful party?'

Pekelis gave him a meaningful stare of widened eyes. An invalid smile perished at the corners of his long pink lips. He looked as gay as a Chekhov heroine. He was tall and willowy with sleek fair hair and long pale hands with slim fingers whose tips were always slightly curled. His dove-grey eyes were as soft as unused razor-blades. His open-necked pastel blue shirt and pale grey suit of imported cloth were far more expensive than anything worn by other men in the cafe. A bright blue silk handkerchief dangled out of his breast pocket like an exhausted acrobat. On one wrist he wore a gold watch which had a broad gold mesh strap and on the other a heavy gold chain like a cable. His brown leather monks were also imported.

As he looked at Silk his eyes seemed to dissolve in steam. He did it jolly well, a fine bit of theatrical business.

Shyly he averted his gaze.

Silk was aware of Martha beginning to bridle.

'I hate large parties,' Pekelis said petulantly. 'All those people! And the noise!' He raised his carefully tended eyebrows. 'They make the air terrible. Sweat and body odours.' His nostrils thinned. 'I prefer a party with a few friends who share the same interests,' he said, returning his gaze to Silk.

Martha Conroy came to the rescue. 'Philip and I were just saying the same thing,' she lied. 'We feel embarrassed by the kindness shown us here. Don't we, Phil?'

'Ah.'

Silk kept his blank gaze fixed on the bulky skin-head figure of Leprechaun who had just seated himself at a table occupied by a man reading *Pravda*.

'We feel awkward about being unable to repay such hospitality. Don't we, Philip?'

'Yes, indeed, Martha.'

Silk saw nothing remarkable about the man at the table chosen by Leprechaun. He was older than most people here. Over the years an inbuilt lawn-mower had cleared most of the hair from his head. He wore dark glasses and a dark suit and an immaculate white shirt with a silver-flecked black tie. He could be any sort of the better-paid Soviet workers. After some moments he folded his newspaper and stood up and left the restaurant flat-footedly. Silk drew a slow breath. That departure suggested his choice of all possible explanations might be correct: the man had relieved Leprechaun for a couple of hours and was now going off-duty. This was no more than the standard treatment for all visiting Western businessmen. Outwardly, he warned himself.

'That is why I came,' Pekelis was telling Martha. He sounded petulant at having to talk to a woman. 'Your friends told me that you and Mr. Foot were here.'

'Oh,' she said in a baffled tone.

'My friends insist you come to a party they are having tonight.'

'Oh it's very kind of you.'

'We seldom have a chance to welcome good friends from Britain.'

'Well, I'd like to come but I don't know if the men are free.'

Pekelis appealed to Silk. 'You will come,' he insisted and his eyes conveyed a significant plea. 'We will have many gay friends there.'

Silk smiled cheerfully, the zahftic Tarzan as Myra Breckinridge would have put it in an off moment. 'I'll ask the others if they think we ought to indulge ourselves instead of working,' he said.

Pekelis moved restlessly. 'Why cannot you come without them?' he asked. 'We would like you to be our guest.'

'We always go out together when we're abroad,' Silk answered. 'It helps us find our way home.' He glanced at his watch and gave an exclamation and stood up. 'We'd better get back. Can you spare the time to walk back to the exhibition with us?'

Behind them a gold-and-green dappled Leprechaun wandered idly.

Hennessy and Keene accepted the invitation without reservation.

Throughout the long hot afternoon they were busy answering questions from parties of trade officials. One came from the Rumanian Embassy, which expressed a hope that the company would exhibit its computers in Bucharest. Another came from the Polish Embassy and wanted to be supplied with diagrams of how the machines worked. After the Poles had gone they raised their brows at each other. Then they met a team of scientists who thought their method of programming might be of assistance on a series of experiments planned for two years ahead.

After the scientists departed they were left alone.

Slowly the afternoon crept on. He did not enjoy being

idle. His nerves began to crawl around like paralytic ants. Although he kept alert for any sign that someone wanted to attract his attention he saw nothing. Inaction, the necessity to remain here on the blasted stand, gradually increased his nerves. City jobs were just not his dish. It needed a peculiar type of mentality to withstand the dragging monotony, the sangfroid of types like Greville Wynne and his sort.

He listened worriedly to the clamour of voices and shuffle of footsteps echoing and re-echoing around this smallest of the Chinese boxes. In one particularly bad moment he felt he had as much chance of survival as a salmon in a poisoned river.

At four o'clock he could take it no longer.

'I'm going for a glass of tea,' he told Keene. 'You coming?'

'Lead on, mate.'

All of them went to the party. Such events were often the equivalent of the capitalist golf-course for concluding business deals. Only Martha welcomed the event. Keene and Hennessy would have preferred a visit to a cinema.

They arrived soon after seven o'clock. It took them some time to locate the apartment block, which turned out to be a recent addition to the concrete forest grown up alongside the Leningrad Highway in the northwest of the city. They had a brief glimpse of the Khimki Reservoir across the road and then their taxi turned right down a side-road towards Degunino suburb and the Dimitrov Highway. They were set down outside a white low-rise block which had eight drab saloon Russian cars strewn in front of its entrance as if for an advertisement photo.

He smelled something phoney about it directly they passed through the open glass doors into a spacious but dark-hued lobby. Although there were no *dvorniks,* house porters, in sight, every detail suggested it was one of those cooperatively owned blocks erected by a committee of higher paid executive workers who put up forty per cent of construction costs.

'Quite snassy,' Hennessy commented, glancing around.

'It's too sombre,' Martha decided.

Silk agreed with her silently. Nonetheless, decor was not everything. His impression that it was a show-place increased. He saw that the carpeting was extremely good, the patterned curtains of good fabric and modern design, the leather couches of excellent quality. Those were unusual features for cooperative buildings whose individual owners were 'granted' an apartment for 'permanent use', a transparent bit of Soviet double-talk. Someone had cared sufficiently to give the lift-doors a touch of elegance. When the cage came to a gentle halt they stepped out into a corridor which had high wide windows and architectural embellishments of a sort of bas-relief of fluted Corinthian columns. They passed gleaming white flat doors set in dull chrome-coloured walls. A good quality green linoleum covered the floors.

Everything convinced him it was phoney. It reminded him of a Zulu kraal he had once visited in the Valley of a Thousand Hills north of Durban, a collection of picturesque rondavels and a quantity of photogenic and heavily beaded girls and engaging mother-naked piccaninns, a tourist erection which bore little resemblance to ordinary Zulu villages he had seen elsewhere up the coast of Natal. This too was a show-place to gull visitors.

They found the flat they were seeking at the far end of a corridor at right angles to the one containing the lift. Behind its white door were convivial voices.

As Silk rang the bell he cringed inwardly as he always did at impending over-exposure to prolonged social chit-chat. Something warned him it would be one hell of an evening. While the others waited he pressed the bell-stud again. At once the door flew open. He bared his fangs delightedly, alarmed by a trampling realization, not for the first time, that the safety of his companions depended on himself.

'Come in, come in!' cried a happy Pekelis. His warm and faintly moist hand seized Silk's like the clasp of a desperate lobster. 'How lucky I was near the door!' He turned to the company beyond. 'Here are our good British friends!'

About twenty people occupied the large square dove-grey walled and lemon carpeted livingroom. They resembled one of those group advertisement photos which sold everything from cars for 'only' so much to Mao Tse-tung's thoughts.

Their British friends were taken around for introductions. All the women were young though the men were of every age. Most of them were strangers though Silk recognized Nina Alexandrovna and Valya Volkova. Nina looked even more devastatingly female in a skin-tight russet silk dress which emphasized every abundant curve and contrasted with the tallow-blonde pallor of silky hair which fell about her shoulders; she was a very *stroinyi zhenshchina*. Her pale grey eyes and prominent lips gave him a smile which could act as a springboard for an eager diver. Volkova gave him a gravely subdued smile. She wore another severe black dress which proclaimed her stated widowhood but did nothing to diminish her aura of frozen sensuality. Her smile implied recognition of mutual attraction. Among others was a slender waif named Sonia with a black urchin cut and a snub nose and huge dark eyes, obviously in her twenties though she could be taken for a twelve-year-old child. Her fascinated gaze reached up to him as if she were overawed by meeting a foreigner. They certainly catered for every variety of male weakness here.

Among the dozen men present were at least three security types. They were Georgi Galanskov, announced as a factory director; Vladimir Demichev, reputedly involved with electrical power; and Sergei Khaustov, from an unnamed planning department. Galanskov was short and rotund, with thinning black hair and eyes half-hidden by rolls of fat in the semblance of a deathless smile.

Demichev was also on the short side but square from wide shoulders to massive buttocks; a quiff of black hair rose from his forehead like the comb of an enraged parrot and his red lips twitched endlessly. Khaustov was tallish and wiry; he had a deeply seamed and tanned face under fair hair and blue eyes as gentle as snake bite. All three oozed affability like plainclothes jacks seconded to special duties. Their feet were probably flatter than an old Bunny girl's charms. Silk began to feel as naked as a peeled egg.

Another individual was a handsome and athletic type with flashing dark eyes and curly black hair who did everything in poses like an old-time movie star. He occupied centre floor, teeth agleam, gaze awander, looking ready to crush the ribs of any wilting wench in impassioned ecstacy. Pekelis introduced him as Sviataslav Streltsov, 'one of our foremost writers' and a dignitary of their Union. Silk imagined he had been hauled in to play on Martha's susceptibilities.

'My British public increases by thousands every year,' Streltsov assured Silk modestly with a disarming smile which did terrible things to the stomach of its beholder. 'They want to read the truth about our Russia.'

That stamped him as a party hack ready to write and say anything to maintain his income and live in his colony far from the world of working Russians. Writers of his sort infested every jungle. You could watch 'em pull out their holy lice. Silk was led willingly away and found himself shaking hands with Strelnikov.

It happened so unexpectedly that excitement coiled coldly round the base of his spine.

'Captain Strelnikov is on leave after being on his ship for six months,' Pekelis cried happily to be heard above the voices which lapped around them. 'Oh, I do love sailors!'

Silk accepted the glass of vodka brought by the huge-eyed waif and felt inclined to agree with Pekelis.

His pleasure was not complete. Several things unsettled him. Strelnikov was taller than he had expected, within an inch or so of six feet. That was tall for a Russian. He was also more thick-set than the photographs showed and there was more grey at his temples. Facially, however, he did resemble the photographs. His high and wide forehead and deep-set grey eyes with their level brows were familiar. So were the straight nose with its wide nostrils and the mobile lips and square jaw. Nothing about his face suggested an Oriental Russian; most of his ancestors were reputed to be French and German and Finnish. What was wholly unexpected was the slanting cheekbone to chin scar down the right side of his face, an old scar too. He must have had it for at least ten years. It had not shown in any of the photographs. Nor had Primakov told them about it.

Silk admitted himself worried.

They chatted amiably amid the hubbub. Strelnikov, or, to be precise, the man introduced as Strelnikov, spoke excellent English. Silk's mind began to fill with unpleasant questions. He delayed giving the recognition signals. His uneasiness was increased by a feeling that the man knew his identity. Those steady eyes had a very knowledgeable glint.

Suddenly Strelnikov said: 'Today my committee intended to visit your exhibition.'

'Your duties must be too exacting for such visits.'

Strelnikov shook his head. 'We have a special interest,' he said. 'We want small computers which can be programmed to our needs. Our own models lack, what is your word? sophistication? Have you something?'

'You know your requirements. Come and see us or send a representative. We will be pleased to demonstrate our models. If I am absent my colleagues will answer any questions.'

He knew he had to play it carefully because if Konuzin were in custody then the real Strelnokov could have been taken too and this man might be a substitute.

'Do you operate a rota?' Strelnikov asked.

'We vary our hours to allow us to see something of your

glorious . . .'

Something bumped Silk sharply and caused his vodka to shower onto the carpet and an alarmed American female voice scurried into apologies.

'Gosh, I surely am sorry,' it said contritely. 'Aren't I just the clumsiest thing you ever did know?'

As Silk looked at her his smile felt like the onset of rigor mortis.

'This is our American friend, Judith Merrin,' Pekelis was telling him. 'Judy's a musical talent scout. She's always visiting us to try to entice away another Ashkenasy or to persuade Richter to tour America. Judy, Mr. Foot is an important businessman. From Britain. Several of his uncles are in the British House of Lords and edit newspapers.'

'Gosh,' she said again, 'we don't need to be introduced, do we, Phil honey? We're old friends. We met up in Berlin and Paris, France. You're taking chances, Phil. You know what these Russians do to you businessmen.'

Silk went on breaking his face. 'They'll cart me off soon,' he agreed in a stage whisper. 'But those Foots or Feet are only poor relations. I'm the rich Foot.'

He thought it likely she would start a scene rightaway which would take all four of them off to await one of those so-called trials staged by the Kremlin. Judith Merrin was neither Judith Merrin nor an American. Her name was or had been Irina Gerina. She was very much a Russian. He had last seen her four years ago outside the house near Sa'na in Yemen just after he had shot and killed Pavel Gerin, her husband. As her spittle ran down his face then she had hissed: 'One day I will kill you, Silk. I will hunt you out until I can shoot you like a dog.'

He had forgotten about her.

9

Beyond the windows the evening light had assumed an acid tinge.

Silk smiled resolutely. It was an occasion for excessive heroism. It only needed the Red Army choir and dance ensemble to blow out their teeth and do cultural cartwheels to turn the whole thing into a wake. Irina's next words increased the fatalities going on among butterflies in his stomach to holocaust dimensions.

'What happened to that stray cat you took for walks?'

He knew when he was beaten.

'I left Tanya with a friend.'

Her widened eyes showed surprise.

'You gave her a Russian name?'

'It has considerable charm.'

'Do you ever see her?'

'No.'

'I guess you couldn't call her a pretty cat.'

'She had so much character she could do without looks.'

Pekelis put another glass of vodka into his hand and took the other one and said cheerfully: 'You old friends must have much to talk about.' He went into the churn of voices and warmth of people's bodies.

She appraised Silk while she sipped her drink. Then she lowered the glass.

'You look fit. Philip.'

'So do you, Judy.'

He had decided even a doomed mouse had a right to stare straight back at the cat playing with it. She clearly intended to pat him around for a bit before she bared her claws. Her reference to Tanya, his gallant and determined companion on a long walk out of Muslim Russia, went back to their first meeting a few years before he killed her husband. On that occasion Gerin had been prepared to leave her alone to die. And he too had left her in a pre-desert to foot-slog after Gerin.

'You haven't changed,' she said sharply.

'You are even more beautiful.'

He nodded at the truth of what he said. When they first met six years ago she was a gypsyish sort of girl of twenty-three, lissom in an old black jersey and black slacks. Abundant coal-black hair had risen steeply above her high forehead and surged like an anchored wave on her shoulders. A lean face, almost triangular, had uniformly level black brows and grey eyes so pale they seemed to be devoid of colour though they could look as if lit by Arctic fire and her lips were pink. One morning he had caught sight of her standing alone on a ridge facing the newly risen sun, Junoesque bosom taut against her jersey, strong capable hands idle at her thighs, an elemental girl clearly able to indulge the wildest passions if the mood seized her but at that instant on the threshold of another day. At that time he had not known she was Gerin's wife.

While he waited for the KGB to surround him he noted she had scarcely changed. Her hair was a shining black coil on the nape of her neck. A scarlet sheen disguised her lips. Her eyebrows had been altered to resemble crescents but those incredible eyes were still watchful. Under the black mini-dress her figure might be a few pounds lighter. Her shapely arms had an assisted dark tan.

Those were minor variations. Beneath them, no one need tell him, was an extremely determined individual. On that distant morning he had thought she had much in common with a snow leopardess, one of his worst similes. He wondered if anyone had tried to tame her since Gerin died. She was not the sort of woman men left alone.

To his surprise she went on making trivial conversation. He indulged her. Evidently she wanted a captive audience on whom to try out her American accent and phrases. Both would have sounded natural from Staten Island to the Golden Gate. All Russian agents were superbly trained in languages and dialects. No hesitation marred her intonation.

He wondered if Kim Philby would join the party. At

present he felt anything might happen. His main concern was what would happen to his companions. There was also the man reputed to be Strelnikov.

'Did you enjoy Berlin?' she asked amusedly.

'It's a fascinating city.'

Her gaze crept round his face as if he were a collector's item. By the nature of their last conversation her expression now should be as triumphant as a fanfare of massed bugles. Yet he saw no glint of derision like Arctic winter sunlight in her eyes. Amid this skirl of voices she might be any attractive girl deliberately prolonging a nothing-natter to suit the occasion.

While he waited he played it her way. Within minutes she must tire of this little game so he filled up his eyes with the last sight of a real female woman he might see for a while and did not disguise the Old Adam watching her. Strangely enough she responded. Neither her voice nor her attitude changed but her eyes suddenly lit up as if brightened by the Northern Lights. Perhaps she intended him to dwell on delights he would soon prefer to forget. He repaid the compliment by giving a lecherous stare calculated to dissolve her knees. For a split second her gaze wavered on the point of sliding away, then met his candidly. It was a neat bit of instinctive female theatrical business. Any onlooker would imagine they were flirting with each other.

'You're looking better than you did, Philip.'

'You always look lovely,' he told her.

'Gosh, Phil honey, it surely is wonderful to see you here.'

Now he could believe her. What spider did not gladly welcome the fly which wandered straight into the web? Fortunately she had lost the seriousness which once kept her madly enthusiastic about beautiful farm-tractors and five-year-plan statistics for the cement or nickel output. So he continued to play it her way but his style.

'You have a rare ability to ensure a man confuses reality with youth,' he said at one point, which was not quite how he phrased it on their walk to the village of Qadamlaqh six summers ago.

She had not forgotten. 'I guess women are bigger fools at that than men,' she said wryly, 'until without warning truth strikes at them and everything else loses meaning.'

It surprised him that she remembered her reply. She even made the words sound new.

He felt beads of sweat trickle down his thighs as a hand gripped his wrist. No malice hardened the warm fingers which played a gentle arpeggio on his wrist. They belonged to Pekelis. His smile seemed to hold only social affability.

'Judy, you naughty American!' he shouted reprovingly. 'Why are you keeping Philip to yourself? Is this another Atlantic Treaty? He must come and drink a toast to the eternal friendship of our great Russia and his Britain.'

She touched his arm. 'Phil honey, come back to me.' she said, almost beseechingly, almost weakly, almost affectionately.

Everyone played their little game or did their thing though he wondered why the devil she bothered.

'I'll be back,' he promised.

There were social evenings and social evenings. This one came under the latter heading. People came, people went. Toasts were drunk to everything except the Chinese leadership. Words had an alcoholic population explosion. Many people talked about their health, proving the rumour that Russians were always on the verge of hypochondria. Out of a thickening haze of cigarette-smoke came shapes which became men or women who stayed long enough to hint at possible future intimacy of some sort if desired, and then went away. This was the routine parade for which a number of visiting non-Russian politicians had fallen. What he did not understand was why they wasted time. There was no need. She had identified him as surely as anyone visiting the morgue.

It foxed him.

After an hour of it their invitations tangled inside his head like steel wool in porridge. It was so damned pointless. This whole elaborate scene, its slick facade of friendliness, its facile conversation, was a waste of effort. They knew him. He was trapped as securely as any luckless creature in a zoo. Did they expect him to foam at the mouth or give shrill whinnies of panic?

Every so often he glanced around for sight of his companions and the reputed Strelnikov. On each occasion he saw them as animated as if they were at a vicarage tea-party. Martha Conroy remained in one corner surrounded by men. To judge from her flushed face she was happier than a film star with a bathful of diamonds.

At the end of another fifteen minutes he decided to go down fighting. He shook off two middleaged gits yawling about fiction as if it were a minuet danced by puppets and not a record of flesh-and-blood people, and set off through the throng to find Pekelis. En route he collided with the bosom of Nina Alexandra, a conflict which only lowered her eyelids as if she and he were speaking *dusha-dashi* soul to soul, as her countrymen put it. He twisted past Strelnikov to where Pekelis was giggling with friends. Pekelis comprehended his requirement immediately.

'Follow me, follow me!' he cried gaily and put down his glass. 'Are you enjoying yourself, my dear friend?'

'It's a gorgeous party.'

They charged through the guests.

'Are British parties so gay?'

'Never quite like this.'

Pekelis led them into and across a drab bedroom devoid of charm or imagination, a thing of brown shapeless furniture and furnishings and yellow paintwork. He opened the door of a bathroom-cum-lavatory whose claim to fame was its size and use as a store-room for household brushes and so on. 'Free on the house, enjoy yourself!' he cried happily and was gone.

When the man who should be Strelnikov came in some

minutes later Silk was washing his hands in the wash-basin.

'Zdravstvuyte!' the Russian exclaimed; 'hello!' He hesitated at the door as if inclined to bolt it, but did not do so. *'Khoroshaya mysl,'* he whispered; 'good idea!' He went across to the lavatory bowl.

Silk saw no cause to leap into Russian. He was still bothered about the scar. And he suspected that every room in this flat was bugged.

'Hello,' he said alcoholically. 'Stuffy in there, in't it?' He gave a squeaky laugh. 'Lov'ly party! Lov'ly women!'

'Noch'yu vse koshka sery,' the Russian said as if to himself: 'at night all cats are grey.' He seemed to regain his wits suddenly and when he spoke his voice indicated a degree of inebriation. 'I'm sorry, Mr. . . Foot, yes? I had forgotten you do not speak our Russian. Are you enjoying the party?'

'Ah, very good.'

'Good,' the man repeated approvingly and turned, buttoning his flies and came across to the wash-basin.

In an oblong horizontal wall-mirror above it, Silk watched the man give the recognition signals which should come from Strelnikov. They were done expertly, seemingly meaningless. He delayed responses, troubled by the scar.

'If I may be personal, Captain,' he said tentatively, 'that is a nasty scar.'

His companion gave him a surprised glance. Then his eyes became shrewd. 'I was in a car accident some years ago,' he said as he began to wash his hands. He gave an abashed laugh. 'I am vain, I always have it taken off my photographs.'

'Mmmm,' Silk said, and then with drunken seriousness: 'Now why?'

'We must not frighten off the women.'

Silk said mmmm again disbelievingly. 'I would have thought they would like it as proof of a mature man,' he said. 'Eh? A warrior. A—a fighter. Mmmm.'

'You may be right, Mr. Foot.'

'Mmmm? Mmmmm. You speak good English. Been to Britain?'

'No.'

Silk picked up the towel from the ice-cold hot rail. 'Anyone'd think so,' he said in an earnest tone. 'Must.' He hesitated. 'Come in spring,' he resumed enthusiastically 'Better'n Paris. See our Post Office To'er, Ric'mon' Park, Fes'ival 'all.' He dropped the towel and stooped to pick it up with his left hand. 'An' Sra'ford-on-Avon.'

Even before he finished speaking the Russian acted. He held out his hands for the towel, wiped them briefly, then slung it round his shoulders and took a comb from an inner pocket. When he had finished he joined Silk out of range of the mirror and gave him a wafer of paper. On it was a brief message in English: 'Meet me in Novodevichy Convent cemetery tomorow at 18:00.'

Silk remembered that the cemetary adjoined the Luzhniki sports complex on a bend of Moscow River.

As he handed back the slip of paper his eyes asked the inevitable question. His companion nodded and rolled the paper into a tiny ball and put it into his mouth and swallowed. That was to say he went through the motions of swallowing and probably did so because the paper was too fragile to withstand moisture. Silk knew that if the whole thing was a ruse to get him to betray himself, then he would soon find out. One fashion and another life had become remarkably complicated this evening.

He and the other man smiled at each other.

That meant damn all. Any man could look sincere if he tried. An accident of birth had given this one inbuilt advantages. His whole face inspired confidence. Those steady grey eyes and mobile lips and the square jaw would sell anything from dud shares to fake religions. One glance at his physique should undermine a class of women psychology students for longer than a term. And he had an aura of clean-living masculine vitality so potent you could nearly smell it. A number of mentally retarded men and murderers, which was the same thing, looked equally dependable. No one here would tell him if he could trust this man.

'We must rejoin our friends,' the Russian said brightly.

'Le'd on, lo'ely par'y.'

As they left the bathroom Pekelis came towards them wearing a petulant scowl.

'Philip, your friend Miss Conway is ill,' he said. His voice edges of annoyance. 'Please come.'

Ill was a polite term for drunk. From every sign, very drunk. She crouched on a chair beside the open window, forlorn as Cinderella. Hair spilled over ringless fingers into which she bubbled misery. Few people paid attention. They knew how vodka made the world appear sad.

Silk bent over her. 'Wha's wrong, Ma'tha?' he said.

'Oh Philip,' she got out, 'is that you?'

'Yes. Wha's wrong?'

'I'm so unhappy. My poor mother . . .'

She rocked perilously from side to side and bubbled wretchedly.

Silk straightened up with the atmosphere of a man pulling himself together unwillingly and in a filthy temper about it. He turned to Pekelis and the man who had been introduced as their host, and whose name he had forgotten because it meant nothing.

'Sorry,' he apologized. 'We should've eaten 'for we came. Your hospital'ty the heat, the noise, mus' have upset her. I'll take her home. In fac', we'd better all go.'

Their host protested angrily. 'No no,' he declared, 'we can keep her here. She will be as good as ever after a little sleep. This party is for you, our good British friends.'

'We'd better go. Work t'do. Mus' get a taxi.'

'Phil honey, I'll glady drive you all back to your hotel,' Irina said. She had come up alongside him unseen. 'Poor thing, she'll be swell directly she's out in the fresh air. It's gotten kinda stuffy here with all these lovely people.' She raised her voice. 'Peke pet, it's been lovely seeing you.

And you, Mr. Afanasyev.'

Silk watched her calm eyes while she spoke. He had seen more positive expression in those of a woman haggling over the cost of a pound of cod. Her lips were twisted into the female smile which meant nothing. Neither indicated the true position. He was still free solely on sufference. Why? His nerves oozed sweat. Logic argued they could not delay his arrest longer than half an hour. Had they gone to the unnecessary lengths of providing themselves with additional evidence by planting incriminating documents in his hotel bedroom? It was possible but seemed a pointless exercize. What the hell were they up to?

'I don't wan' t' spoil your fun, Judy,' he said sincerely.

She gave him another female smile, the sort of smile young girls practised at a mirror for hours to dazzle everyone. 'Phil honey,' she said, 'you won't. They'll see me again soon. You boys bring her down carefully while I get the auto ready.'

When he rejoined Irina in the hotel lobby he felt like a captive rabbit. In the twenty minutes or so since he left her he had managed to get into all their bedrooms. They were empty of other people. If fake evidence had been planted in his room it was in a very unusual place. Everything suggested another plan was being followed.

As he crossed the lobby he glanced round. Girl receptionists chattered behind their desk. Most visitors were familiar to his eyes. A raven-haired Indian girl in a pink sari murmured to herself. An exuberant East German family shouted at each other as if they had just been reunited in Heaven. Two Nassah-moustachioed Egyptians gave a connoisseur's attention to every pair of legs leading to a female pelvis. A grey-haired Polish trio which he had seen on other evenings had regrouped with heads close together like film conspirators. There was only one newcomer, a big blonde woman who sat straight upright like a kinky doll and whose china-blue eyes stared vacantly ahead; he had half a mind to go over and press her navel to see if she said 'Mama.' Beyond her was a group of African diplomats in their Savile Row suits and white collars.

Irina looked up from the magazine on her lap as he halted beside her. Her smile was intended to unite them in mutual oblivion of nearby humans. Or so he assumed. Since their last encounter she had become a good actress. Any stranger seeing her now could be excused if they assumed her to be a normal woman in that stage of love when she feels at ease only if the object of her affection is with her. He flashed his teeth.

'How is she?' she asked, and her voice held relief.

'Better. She'll be all right after a rest. It was kind of you to bring us back. Would you like a drink?'

She smiled and laid the magazine aside and stood up.

'Let's go for a drive,' she suggested, and contrived to sound as eager as a girl. Impulsively her hand seized his. 'It's too lovely an evening to waste.'

He did his best to resemble a happy man not conscious of being taken for a ride by the KGB. This was, as his American friend Hank Luce would say, an occasion to keep his cool. He smiled back at her.

'My friends may fret if I go without telling them. Not that they have any cause. They don't know how I spend my spare time.'

'I understand.'

'I'm a free agent. They are not responsible for me.' Once upon a time the very idea of a beautiful Russian spy had been more than a giggle: their spy-masters left physical enticement to German women like Marie and Hungarians and Poles, working them as arduously as now, in another fashion, they let little Arab boys be slaughtered in their bid to control the Middle East. Yet Irina here, working her home town, surrounded by fellow-members of the KGB, probably listening to a microphone concealed somewhere on her which caught the sound of their voices, plus millions of indoctrinated little friends, with plainclothes *druzhinniki*, members of the *drushiny*, volunteer civilian police, thick as flies on a dead camel, in every football and athletics and swimming audience and cinema; with help on every side, Irina elected to display feminine charm in a style calculated to revive their memories of each other.

'*Vam skutchno*?' she whispered gently; 'are you bored?'

'*Nyet nyet*.'

She smiled.

'*Nu, idyom, da*?; well, let's go, yes?'

He decided instantly. At least the others could plead total ignorance when they discovered he had gone missing.

'*Da, ya poida 's tobaq*; I will accompany you.'

As they walked to the entrance she exclaimed happily: 'Gosh, it's good to see you again, Phil. I had just gotten kinda lonesome. You know how it is.'

'I do, yes.'

They drove across the river and canal. Few cars used the streets now though thousands of people were out enjoying a stroll in the cool air of a tranquil warm evening. High above the city a single miles-long feather of lacey cloud floated under the higher blueness. Irina maintained her role of an American while she drove, recalling incidents of their supposed recent meeting in Berlin. Certainly she had either been there at the same time as himself or someone had genned her up. He took this part of the conversation to mean she wanted to gain a morsel of career-status on front of whoever was listening to the microphones concealed somewhere in the car. In the circumstances he saw no logical cause to deny her any kudos she sought. His invented recollections caused her to laugh up and down the scale of amusement.

At Dobryninskaya Square she turned left. Soon afterwards he saw the distinctive modern-style upper floors of the Warsaw Hotel ahead and they came to Oktyabrskaya Square at the north end of Gorki Park. Around this region the ponderous magnificence of central Moscow ebbed and the drabber areas took over.

When he agreed to her suggestion that they go for a walk in the park she found a convenient parking space on Krymsky Val Street. He got out wondering if he was to be given the fatal accident treatment or whether this was to be the setting for where she would shoot him down like a dog as she had sworn to do.

As they went towards the main entrance he glanced back and saw two solid weightlifter types in worn grey suits get out of a car which had slowed to a halt only a short distance behind the one they had just left.

Irina kept strictly to social chat until they were beyond the pavilion and walking between trees towards the boating-station and stands alongside the river. She was a beautifully erect woman, moving gracefully though without affectation. Suddenly she gave a sharp exclamation and clutched his arm for support while she shed a shoe. Holding onto him she regained it and shook it vigorously. No chip of stone fell out. She put it on again. He did not ask the question which came to his mind.

Walking on, she asked curtly: 'Are those two men behind us?'

'Which men?'

'Those men from the car. I knew you would look if I gave you a chance. I do not think they are interested in us, but no one can be sure in Moscow. They think you will talk more candidly to an American woman you already know.'

'Which car, Judy?'

She gave a sound of annoyance and started to turn her head.

'No,' he told her.

Her cold fingers threaded among his and she led them down a tree-lined path away from those favoured by other people. When she was sure they were briefly unseen she stopped, pulling him round to face her. Her raised eyes had lost their social glint.

'Search me,' she ordered bleakly. 'I shall not scream.'

He did so as thoroughly as circumstances permitted. As he did so she closed her eyes and her lips tightened.

'Right,' he agreed. 'Either you do not have a bug on you or it is of a type unknown to me. Anyway, let's stop playing games. Here I am. What now?'

She opened her eyes. 'There is not a bug,' she told him as if uttering a vow. 'Do you believe me? I love the feel of your hands.'

He stared at her incredulously. 'Thank you,' he said dazedly. 'I should believe you?'

'*O Bozye moi*!' she said exasperatedly. At once she looked round to see if they were unobserved and, satisfied, she looked at him, smiling. '*Moi vozlyublyyanni*' Dorian. *Ya vaz nuzda.*' She raised her face. '*Myenya potsyelui, moi lyubi*——' Her voice caught, breaking the endearment.

He had never expected her of all possible women to think of him as her beloved Dorian, to say she needed him, to think of him as her darling, or to ask him to kiss her.

Life was full of surprises.

10

Silk had always subscribed to the basic principle that an agent should keep his priorities right. For himself at present these were to get the information if it was forthcoming from the man who claimed to be Strelnikov and to find out if he could about Konuzin and to get his innocent colleagues and himself out of Russia alive. Those were realities. Nothing else mattered. Every difficulty which arose unexpectedly had to be dealt with as it arose from the viewpoint of enabling him to keep his grasp on the realities. He had to keep mobile for as long as he could in order to ensure he could fulfil each stage of the mission entrusted to him. That was part of the tradition of the service. So he played it on the lip.

It put his defences under a quite unexpected strain. She hung onto him as if someone had just borrowed her lovely long long legs and taken them away. She beseeched him silently to forget the problems of their universe and concentrate on what psychologists call tactile stimulation, the delights to be felt as their bodies pressed upon each other and their mouths conjoined as if their lungs had endured oxygen starvation for a decade and their frustrated hands guessed at wild delights to be found if they could gain a palpation of erogenous zones. By golly, it was unexpected. True, he was a gorgeous beast and all that but no one on her side of the accidentally inherited argument had ever swooned or torn their hair out at a glimpse of his classic features and Mr. Universe statistics. They saved it for more profitable prospects. She clung to him as if she had not lived since they last saw each other. Ooooh, she wanted something special. Oh yes she did.

He thought of icebergs and kept his cool.

After a long restless contact Irina drew her head back. *'A . . . a, nyen'nyi,'* she muttered huskily. *'Nakonyets'to . . . eto nashe schast'ye!*; at last . . . we are lucky!' She kept her eyes shut while she let him see her smiling-stunned face. That meant precisely nothing. It played a part in the female appeasement schedule. Then she laid her face against his shoulder and beyond her a man who was gazing at them darted behind a tree. It was not Leprechaun. Her fingers crept testingly up his arms as if to ensure he had biceps.

'I have waited a long time to let you know I am yours,' she said in a thick unsteady voice. 'Did you bring a gun?'

He saw the man's head pop into and out of sight. There was something unpleasantly familiar about the face. 'No,' he said. 'Why should I have a gun? I've retired. There's more money in business. Perks too.'

She laughed indulgently. 'You will never retire, my darling,' she said in a dreamy voice, 'and we may need a gun.' She tightened her hold as she sensed him about to release her. 'No no, darling love, hold me just a little longer,' she entreated. '*Ne nada*; don't punish me. It is so good to hold you in my arms and feel you against me after the years of wanting you, the man.'

Quite obviously she did want something and it wasn't the sort of hour when any man would fuss about what it might be. She sounded like a page out of *War and Peace.* This treatment represented a distinct variation from usual methods of shearing locks off a capitalist Samson, and fine obsessive stuff it was too, but he knew damn well it had nothing to do with his magnificent powers of attraction. This could be her version of the mink coat gambit. It would be ungentlemanly not to enjoy it. 'Irina,' he said and his voice throbbed. He kissed the top of her head like a sailor homecoming after being alone on an island for years. It gave him a chance to watch for Peeping Ivan. She moved restlessly against him.

'I want to go to bed with you,' she murmured. Her open mouth pressed against his shirt. 'We may have to kill someone before we go. I will get you a gun.'

He was busy. Peeping Ivan had reappeared, the left half of him, trying to get a clear sight of the enraptured pair. He was about five feet six tall and forty years old, but an old forty, and of stocky physique. His white sports shirt needed love and his dark trousers had lost elegance. Something about his pale Russian face with its high cheekbones, blunt nose, and Asian eyebrows, kept chiming on memory. He vanished like a Walt Disney squirrel.

While Silk kissed her hair he sent his memory sniffing back across the years. Within seconds it started to return to him, retrieving something. Seven or eight years ago. Jordan, near Amman. Then it pitched a name into his mind. Viktor Zakharov.

This really was not his evening.

Irina freed her head to raise her face. Her pale eyes seemed to blaze at him. Their plea was unmistakable.

He thought it would be churlish to deny either of them when he wanted a chance to think. Fortunately both of them possessed strong legs. She trembled at his ardour.

Seven or eight years ago Zakharov and he had met when an order from London sent him to discover what plot the Kremlin was hatching among marsh Arabs of the Shatt al-Arab at the junction of the Tigris and Euphrates. In those days a ferocity of Russian determination to turn the Middle East into its colonial playground by appealing to illiterate Arabs through using puppet guerrillas who played on fanatical Arab nationalism was just beginning to cause weak and meekly pious do-gooder British politicians to scuttle out of the region. Zakharov and he had circled around each other like belligerant butterflies, amid village *mudhifs* and their *mashufs*, canoes, and Zakharov had lots of money, the real *baqsheesh,* to win favour. Zakharov had in tow a *dhakar binta,* a dancing boy prostitute with wild dark eyes and a willowy body. When they tried to kill him one night outside Amman they had only just escaped themselves because Zakharov too had run out of ammunition. Zakharov, a KGB man, tended his memory like other men tended their roses. He had not forgotten even though his moustache was greyer now.

Obviously he was either here in the capacity of one attending an identity parade or had blundered on this romantic scene. Whatever the cause for his presence, his attention was focused on them. It would be unfriendly.

Irina freed her head. 'Darling,' she said with breathless delight.

'Foolish girl,' he said fondly.

She accepted his intention not to go on and leant back against his arm. 'Not a girl, only an archetypal woman,' she confessed. 'Yours since the moment you killed Gerin. No other man has possessed me. *A . . . a, vsyo khorosho chto khorosho konslopetsya;* all well, ends well.'

'You threatened to kill me like a dog.'

'Try to understand. It was a natural reaction. Our marriage was arranged by the KGB. We did not share love. But our bodies knew each other's needs.'

'You knew what I was.'

She smiled strangely. 'I am also like those women of ancient Greece,' she said. 'They became the loyal women of men who killed their husbands. Many women here do not marry men they love. It is a business contract. Our increasing divorce rates prove it. But every Russian woman hungers for romantic love. I tried to love Gerin. When he left me in that desert I knew we were not even comrades.'

'I also left you there.'

'You had no alternative,' she said without rancour. 'You said I might put a bullet into your head if you fell asleep. Since then I too like many others here have thought much about what our country does. No, what its rulers do. You became my truth.'

He saw Zakharov take another look at them. From the way he narrowed his eyes he might be trying to identify Irina from her back.

'Now this is becoming too involved,' he said.

'It is simple. Until they told me you were a British spy I believed only our agents had sufficient courage to penetrate enemy territory. We are trained to believe only our agents are brave. Men like Richard Sorge, Rudolf Abel, Valentin Alexandrovich Pripolzev, the Krogers as you call them, men and women of our Great Patriotic War, men like Domb—'

'And Trepper and his associates.'

'Yes. I realized there are many men like you, perhaps thousands, but you are the one I knew.'

'So?' he prompted.

Her voice came falteringly as if unsure of his reaction to her words. 'That night after you killed Gerin my body ached for you,' she said. 'Was it so strange? It would have been right for us to lie together and share our living. You are only the man who fired the shot. It could have been, it would have been, another man somewhere later. It was you. We should have given each other solace amid the turmoil our rulers invent in order to gain mastery of the world. Now Brezhnev wants to dominate a servile Europe as he has dominated and cowed Czechoslovakia. Such men deserve to die. We can work towards that end. This fire in us for each other will sustain us.' Her voice had gained strength. 'I am yours not only because you won me in combat but because I want to be yours,'

His mind was a bit fussed. What she said about the women of ancient Greece came from more than the work of playwrights who followed Aeschylus at the Dionysian festival, and applied to other women too, but he needed a chance to think about it. His thoughts did a back somersault.

'You mentioned a gun,' he said cautiously.

'So I can come with you or we can die together for freedom,' she said without hesitation. 'We will be martyrs for mankind if we cannot be crusaders for freedom and justice.' She kissed his shirt again. 'You read my note, the one I slipped into your pocket near the History Museum this morning. It was clever of you to pretend not to see me. My love, watch.'

While he watched he thought it most unclever not to have seen her. Glancing round, she went back a step and performed the signals which Konuzin should have given to establish his identity. He did nothing to stop her; the signals meant nothing to an onlooker unless he knew them. If Zakharov knew them he knew them. Period. It could mean that Konuzin had been tortured into betrayal and she had been entrusted to catch him. He felt ice lumps tinkling in his stomach.

As she straightened up her eyes were shining. 'Darling?' she said.

'Ah-ha.'

'I have the information the Professor intended to give you. And much more. He is one of my oldest friends.'

'Ah, of course. And you said we met in Berlin.'

Her hands fondled his jacket sleeves. 'I was there,' she said. 'That whore Helga Pohl reported to me to pass the information on to her director. She did not know who you are. Nor does he. They think you are a weak man who can be blackmailed by a woman.'

'What man isn't?'

Her eyes took on a green expression without attaining the hue. 'Did she haul you into her bed?' she asked bitterly. *'Chyortova kykla, yavno propashchiye;* silly bitch, quite hopeless. She serves the KGB well. Did you find her attractive?'

'Would any man like her?'

'You took her to London.'

'She had business there,' he agreed, knowing it useless it deny it. 'She merely asked if she could travel with me. After we reached London I put her down in the West End for her to go and see a friend. I haven't seen her since.'

Irina smiled. His answer seemed to have satisfied her. 'She is not a nice woman,' she said gently in Russian. Her quietness damned Marie worse than any outburst. 'I have a full knowledge of her work. One thing she does not know. I do. When we get to Britain I will tell you the identity of Jeremy.'

'Jeremy,' he said thoughtfully and tried not to sound surprised. ' . . . Jeremy?'

'Ne prickyd' vaisya, pazhalsta,' she protested; 'don't pretend, please.'

'I suppose he told you I am here.'

She shook her head. 'He sent information that you were coming,' she said. 'I destroyed it. Later he said you would not be coming and we should leave your team alone. When I went to the exhibition I did not expect to see you. No one else knows you are here.'

He was most unimpressed. 'My firm thought I was going to have a dose of Asian 'flu,' he said. 'It's playing unseasonal tricks this year.' He reached up his hand and smoothed the fingers down her firm cheek. 'It's wonderful to see you. What you say is right. I never forgot you.'

'I always wanted you.'

Nothing in her smile gave him any clue as to whether she was telling him the truth. Some things she had said appeared to be unnecessary if they intended to snatch him; her words had put him on his guard. What she said might be inspired by what the Russians called *blat*, a generic term for 'influence', covering everything from wire-pulling to blackmail. He smiled at her.

'Stay like that,' he told her. 'You really are a smasher, you always were, but now, boy, gorgeous. Do you know Viktor Zakharov?'

A frown plucked at her forehead. 'He works in one of our departments,' she answered. 'Do you know him? He was in the Middle East.'

'Right now he's part of a tree behind you. He's trying to recognize you.'

He saw flickers of tension along her lips and eyelids. They were natural. He reached an arm forward to circle her waist and bring her close. She had a genuine female waist, not one of those starved boy affairs.

'*Krasioyi stroinyi zhenshina,*' he complimented her. 'He failed to kill me one night.'

'Has he recognised you?'

'He's not playing dwarfs or elves over there.'

'Kiss me while I think,' she said. After some seconds she freed her mouth. 'Has he gone?'

'. . . *nyet.*'

She gave an uncharacteristic laugh.

'Behind you on the left is a path. It will take us to near where I left the car. We will be lucky, my darling. We are together. At last.'

They walked on talking animatedly about nothing.

Nobody paid much attention to them. To every outward sign they were just another man and woman who enjoyed each other's company and were at peace together on a quiet family walk through the warm evening. This lack of interest could change in seconds to violent hostility so he kept mentally adjusted. Once he stooped to retie a shoe-lace. Zakharov was close behind, suddenly absorbed by thoughts scattered over the ground. There was no sign of the two men who had got out of the car.

They might be in a *kafe* enduring the long wait for a glass of *chai* or bottle of *peva*; Muscovites told bitter jokes of people dying of thirst or starvation while waiting in their eating houses. His mind searched around for a pause from confusion.

As they went on she slid her strong fingers between his and matched her stride to his in loving unity. And once upon a time there were three bears.

'He may not be sure it is you,' she said quietly.

'True. I haven't got a memorable face.'

'It will always be young and fresh in my memory.'

'You're a devil for punishment.'

'No, only a typical Russian woman. All of us will take endless risks for those we love. You will learn.'

'Sentimentalist.'

'So are you, caring for that stray cat,' she responded fondly. 'I hope we can get away from Zakharov. He may not have a car. If only we could spend the night together. A man needs proof of his woman's need of his body.'

'It would be unwise.'

'Yes, we must be discreet. You cannot come to my hotel room. Your room is bugged. So is every hotel room in Russia. Whenever the doors open an electric switch turns on a tape-recorder which is in what they call a staff-room on the same floor. And every tape is listened to within a short time.'

'What a world!'

'We must be patient, my darling. Soon we will have outwitted them.'

Ominously, few people were in sight as they rounded an exhibition pavilion and the main entrance came into view beyond the trees. Only a straggle of people were leaving the park; they looked like families who would walk or travel home by the Metro. Nobody was entering it. Those signs could mean anything. At this hour most people here were either in the theatre or dance-hall or sports stadium or one of the several *kafes*. It could mean that people had been cleared in order for battle to commence.

Irina let go of his hand. He stepped a couple of paces away from her.

His heart was beating a bit faster as they emerged unchallenged on the other side of the main gates.

No one near displayed interest in either himself or Irina. Nobody came towards them. They were all going leftward towards the bridge and the Metro station beyond it. Irina talked like a well-trained New Yorker, used to quicker restaurant service. He listened to a quickened breathing in their wake.

An angry voice said: 'Silk. Dorian Silk. Irina Gerina.'

Neither of them paid attention.

'Phil, do you remember the week we spent in Boston?' Irina asked, loudly enough for Zakharov to overhear. 'Gosh, what fun! I wish we were there, honey.'

'Me too,' he agreed with feeling.

'Silk!'

They were laughing too happily to heed the grim voice.

'Where shall we go, Phil?' she asked as they reached the car. 'Would you like to come to my place?'

'There's nothing I'd like better.'

Something small and hard and unfriendly shoved the left side of his back. He gave a sound of startlement. She reacted immediately.

'What is it?' she asked, and then, went on worriedly: 'Who are you?'

He swung round. His movement knocked aside the hand at his back. It did contain an automatic. Instantly it swung back to point at his stomach. Zakharov's eyes had an expression of certainty. He smiled tightly.

'Dorian Silk,' he said, and his voice gloated.

'Judy, don't panic,' Silk said. 'It's a hoodlum.'

Zakharov glared at him. Since they last saw each other his face had became more noticeably Russian. Those eyebrows would nest birds; his cheeks had a rubbery fullness. At three feet off his breath still made the smell of camels seem like something dreamed up by Chanel.

'It long time been,' he was saying excitedly. 'Together met we often many times until you I prevented from killing me.' His gun waved like a chorus girl's fan. 'So trying our Soviet fatherland to destroy yes? with this this *zhenshena* ah wo-man! our workers seduce yes?'

Silk had once doted on an Aunt with a similar affliction. Whenever invited into one of those houses which kept a piano stabled in the livingroom she would sing. Bosom adrift, hair atumble, cadence like a ride on a fairground switchback, on she plunged, littering the Shalimar with pale hands and demanding that God bless this house. Zakharov just had to mangle English.

'Phil honey, is this person a friend of yours?' Irina asked coolly.

'A stranger. And off his rocker.'

Zakharov choked on annoyance. He understood the language better than he spoke it. 'Silk you, Dorian, for Britain a spy,' he hissed. *Da!'*

'No.'

"Da da! Da!'

'Please don't try to establish a relationship. My name is Foot.'

'Silk!'

'And this is Miss Judy Merrin of New York. We are here on business.'

'Silk!'

'Please put that little thing away.'

'Silk!'

'Do you want roubles to buy a new record? Foot.'

Silk had turned his bored face from side to side. None of the people in sight paid attention to them. Each had more important things on their mind than one man who talked loudly and used extravagant gestures in this city where many gesticulated. They probably dismissed him as one of the country's millions of drunkards. On the other hand, as Silk had witnessed in Berlin and London, nowadays lots of people did not want to get involved. Here most people were terrified of attracting official attention.

He smiled at Irina. 'Get into the car,' he told her. 'This may be a long business. Our friend has been at the vodka.'

'I'm staying with you, my darling. He's dangerous.'

As she spoke the automatic dug into Silk's stomach. One section of his mind could almost see the gang-plank being lowered from the big ship to let a late passenger run up and claim his berth in the stern. He also reckoned it would be better to die quickly and alone rather than have the glaring lights and methods of talk-inducement favoured by the KGB.

Opening his lips as if to speak, the side of his left hand chopped down on the wrist of the hand which held the gun. It knocked the weapon aside as Zakharov tried to steady it. He expected to hear at least one shot caused by an involuntary tightening of the trigger finger. A split second later he expected it again as he grabbed hold of Zakharov's hand and wrenched it back towards the forearm. No shot came. Instead two swift heavy blows on the jaw from the other man's fist rocked his head. Black flags waved wildly in front of eyes. He guessed one of the Russian's knees was coming up to get acquainted with a vital section of his anatomy. It failed to find its goal but delivered a heavy thump inside his right thigh. Another blow set his head ringing with a carillon of unmerry jingle bells.

None of it affected his intuition. He was positive now that Zakharov was carrying an unloaded automatic. His steadily increasing grip succeeded. He heard a long moan of pain as he finally forced the Russian to release the weapon. As his vision returned to normal he struck the man a sharp open-handed blow on the side of the neck. Without a sound the Russian sagged and toppled, hitting the back of his head as he fell against the car and then spread across the ground. At once he stooped to get the automatic and pocketed it.

Irina had kept her wits. 'Quickly, get him inside,' she whispered urgently. 'No one is watching.' And he hoped that proved whose side she was on.

He did not question her advice. Together they got Zakharov into the back and propped him up against the side as if half asleep.

A sudden tide of people swirled out of the park as Irina got into the driving seat. Within the ten seconds it took him to get back to the other side, several hundreds of them spilled out across the pavements. By far the greatest number came towards them, hurrying towards the bridge. He got in beside her and saw the question in her eyes.

'Can we drive round for a bit?' he asked. 'It's a lovely evening.'

'Whatever you feel like, honey.'

Their passenger slept too deeply to join in the conversation.

Half an hour later she pulled up on a deserted tree-lined strip of road on the main highway to Minsk. They had talked gaily and continuously at first to cover any voice behind them.

It was getting dark. Buildings they had left behind them had windows which were vertical lozenges of light. Few cars or long-distance lorries had tried to poison them with clouds of exhaust. Nevertheless there were people nearby and every few minutes a car or homeward-bound bicyclist passed them. Some distance ahead a geometric scatter of pale lights amid intense blackness under a fading turquoise sky with frothy bars of yellow radiance showed the next main area of housing.

Neither of them spoke as they got out. Irina came to stand silently beside him while he opened the rear door. His examination did not take long. Their unspoken fears about any sound or movement were justified. Zakharov must have been awkwardly placed for that blow on the neck or when he hit the car as he fell. He was as dead as anyone who died B.C.

11

He wished there had been long enough intervals between these various shocks to let him get his breath and decide what to do. At his own pace. This rush of events prevented any chance to plan logically. As Swann, his old tutor, had often told him, covert warfare requires continual pliability. Swann never spoke truer words. It also demanded endless resilience of spirit, a conviction of being able to leap uphill indefatigably and with a sweet-scented rose between the faultless teeth, en route to total victory and a football club's substitute for holy water, a bottle of champagne. And when an instant perfect decision is also required on how to dispose conveniently of the mortal remains of an enemy government's official in the enemy's capital city—and Russia had shown herself to be the enemy of every country which did not follow her style of politics—a host of other unusual qualities were essential. Minor attributes like remarkable courage and resourcefulness and confidence and commonsense and genius, simple things like that. Plus on this occasion faultless insight into the mind of this one of all possible women.

He was appalled by his lack of the skills necessary for this situation.

Zakharov had been most inconsiderate to die off like this.

His living companion remained silent. That might mean or signify only her professional curiosity about how another agent would operate in these circumstances. For all he knew the trap would still be sprung on him. Soon. Her silence could indicate astonished pleasure that chance had given her such help. He wished he knew what thoughts occupied her mind. From his point of view the incident had only one good feature. Zakharov had not had a chance to talk to the listening microphones while inside the car.

'Fine!' he exclaimed cheerfully. 'How much cooler the air is now, isn't it?'

He shut the door.

As he heeled round he took her arm and led her across into the shadows. No near sound came from the darkness gathering around them. He had forgotten how quiet Moscow could be at night, away from the haunts of its drunks. Momentarily it helped him in an attempt to think above the pace of events. This bade fair to become one of the longest evenings of his life.

He found that she was not as indifferent as he had believed. As they stopped he realized she was trembling and breathing unsteadily. Instantly he kissed her lips to see what they might tell him. They were cold and weak but tried to respond as if she wanted the reassurance of living contact. On an assumption that she might be genuinely shocked, he tried to quieten her. It gave him a chance to quieten himself. Gradually the trembling against him began to subside.

Her reply to his question was expected.

'I was so happy,' she muttered. 'Women cannot be indifferent to death.'

He had heard the thought expressed through similar words in a score of bad plays. It was open to scrutiny. Nonetheless, while this mood was upon her, she could mean it. Russian emotions were still basically early nineteenth-century romantic if earthy. He postponed judgment. Everything pointed to the next few minutes being crucial in one respect. Events forced him to rely on instinct, a great many agents of every country had died because their instructors paid no attention to psychology. But he wished he had given himself more exercize in prayer.

'Do you think someone told him to follow us?' he asked.

'Why should he try to arrest you alone if he had others to help him?'

'He acted rashly.

'He was surprised to see you. He thought only of stopping the car.'

'My memory suggests he would act more logically. He could have taken the number of your car.'

'He had a nervous breakdown. For the last two years he has done only office work. He drank.'

'You knew him.'

'He knew me. There is a difference.'

Essentially, her quiet voice told him nothing. It had the level tone of an intelligent woman sharing a calamity with a man who gave her confidence.

'I wonder why he didn't speak to you,' he said.

Irina gave a humourless laugh. 'He knew I am never assigned to duties which require me to make love in public,' she told him. 'He saw how I kissed you, my darling. No one has ever seen me kiss a man. Pavel believed it was unhygenic.'

'Oh.'

She threaded cold fingers among his. 'Even a village idiot can detect a woman in love quicker than the man she loves,' she said and her voice held a thread of laughter. 'Do I sound like poor Khrushchov with one of his rustic parables? All Russians are afflicted by it. We are close to the earth. Her tone hardened. 'Zakharov was no fool. Only politically immature. Perhaps that is another of our national weaknesses. What are we going to do about his body?'

He had been afraid she might ask that.

'Was he married?

'No.'

'I thought the KGB liked its agents to be married.'

'Only if they do not have a family which can be disgraced to warn other agents and their families what to expect if they become anti-Kremlin. It is better if an agent has memories of a wife whose body he has penetrated and whose weaknesses he wants to believe only he will know. Our KGB, like the Czars' Oprichniki, believes in an exercize of tyranny through the exploitation of fear.'

'Zakharov had a family?'

'A mother, two brothers and their wives, three sisters

and their husbands. I think he had nine or ten nephews and nieces.'

'At one time he liked Arab boys.'

'No one knew.'

'I saw him with one frequently. What about his father?'

'An old Bolshevik who died before the war.'

He went tense as a car whined into sight farther down the road and zig-zagged crazily towards them. Someone inside it sang the latest Moscow pop song at the top of a discordant baritone, which might or might not prove drunkenness. He swung her round and kissed her mouth. She responded like a vow, stilled inside the arm he kept round her waist. Every so often the beam of the headlights from the nearing car swept over them. Then it slowed down, and her sudden tension proved it was not a trick of his imagination. It went past, leaving a trail of unmusical voice which gradually withered against his ear. He kept his arm round her waist.

'If only you knew how I have hungered to feel your strong body against mine and could understand the desire you awake in me,' she muttered in Russian, and then, reluctantly, asked: 'Why are you interested in Zakharov?'

'I need to know something about him. Did he always do everything to a fixed routine? Outside of office hours?'

Irina was silent for a moment, leaning back on his arm, her thighs braced against his, and finally her head gave a negative shake.

'None of us risk being friendly with each other. Friendship is impossible. People may fall out of favour or be stigmatized as anti-party conspirators or personality cultists. Nobody knew Zakharov well. After his breakdown he developed a violent temper. Drink did not help it.'

'He had enemies.'

'Yes.'

'Departmental feuds.'

'There are always personal feuds in the KGB. It has no true *esprit de corps,* except among those outside of Russia. He always boasted about his father being an Old

Bolshevik, one of those who won the revolution.'

'He was a Stalinist.'

'Yes. With a grudge because he believed he should be more important, because of his father.'

'Was he a Party aristocrat?'

'Our Old Bolsheviks are like American film cowboys and your footballers. Here today and forgotten tomorrow. Folk heroes. Not aristocrats.'

'Why was he unpopular?'

Irina took a deep breath. 'I am better now because you are so calm,' she said. 'Younger members do not like to learn that many Old Bolsheviks murdered defenceless people needlessly and without even the type of trial which disgraces our Russia today. Zakharov's father ordered the execution of nearly six hundred people whose only crime was that they did not believe in communism.'

'Tell me.'

'He was commandant of a labour camp of liberal scholars who refused to support Lenin. After he had them shot he told Moscow they had mutinied. A son of one of the scholars murdered him a week or two after Stalin had named him a Hero of the Soviet Union.'

'Mmmm . . . do you know where he lived?'

'He had an apartment in a block in Davydkovo suburb.'

'We passed it on our drive here.'

'Yes. He was lonely and must have walked in Gorki Park after supper.'

Another car came towards them. It came from the opposite direction and could be the same one. A long slight curve of the road fastened its headlights on his face. A second car followed it. Irina kept close to him.

When the cars disappeared she drew back but held onto his shoulders.

He ignored her question. An idea had come to him; not before time. All this litter of indigestible official architecture and city streets inhibited him; such things always did, anywhere on this overpopulated and despoiled orange of a planet. Such places increased every risk a thousandfold. A body could not be left around without cause. Someone might tell the police they had seen Zakharov and the car. He had to take a risk.

'What districts were we going towards?' he asked, breaking into something she was saying about being *otzyvchivy*, full of sympathetic response to him, and how they were *chutley*, the Russian word for *sympathique*.

'Tatarovo . . . Khoroshevo-Mnevnicki . . . Strogino. Tushino and Bratsevo are farther on.'

'Are they built-up districts?'

'Not completely.'

'Are there country roads there?'

'Several.'

They were speaking Russian, their voices lowered, and she went on to use the word *rasputitsa,* the springtime roadlessness of many rural areas due to the floods and mud of April.

'And they have blocks of flats.'

'Yes.'

'What sort of people occupy them?

'Professional and managerial workers and their families. I have a woman friend who lives in a *stolelnaia kvartira,* separate apartment, in Tatarovo. The block was a *zhilishchno-stroitelnyi kooperativ,* housing-construction cooperative.'

'One of those places which are allowed if the tenants find a large part of the building cost.

'Yes.'

While the idea gained shape he took the opportunity to mix pleasure with business. It lacked the first fire but Irina ensured it was pleasurable. She might be abundantly willing. What did it mean? Others had delighted in head-hunting, to use an aphorism. One of them was Catherine the Great, a description which politely left off the adequate final noun. Among her energetic mates was at least one of the Orlov brothers, possibly three, probably as a reward for deposing and murdering her ineffectual husband; also the imperialistically-minded Potemkin, and

Poniatowski who strove mightily to become king of the vassal state of Poland. Zavodovsky, who else? Oh, Zoritch, Korsakov, Lanskei, the impetuous bigot Zubov who was thirty years younger than herself, dozens who had her for a night or a weekend, a mare of a woman. Many Russians were proud of their German princess Catherine.

As often happened when he thought of something trivial, unimportant to whatever he was doing, his idea suddenly flowered.

Irina freed her mouth. 'You are driving me mad with need,' she muttered.

'What do you think you are doing to me?' he asked, and added, with some truth: 'I long to know you are mine.'

'I will be, I will be. What are we going to do?'

'There is only one thing we can do,' he said, and drew her back towards the car. 'We had better get it done quickly. I'll drive. Answer me as if you were driving.'

They found a deserted side road between a nest of newish apartment blocks and a Metro station on the Molodyozhnaya line. A straggle of night-black trees and bushes bordered it on either side. No street light illuminated it though he could see from the road surface that it was in frequent use. By day-traffic only, he felt inclined to pray.

Irina left this part of it entirely to him. She maintained her American impersonation, following his conversational leads with a slight delay as if preoccupied with driving.

'Are we lost?' he asked as he slowed down.

'Guess so, honey. This is unfamiliar to me.'

'Pull in. I'll ask someone how we get back to the Kremlin.'

She laughed. 'Are you going to visit with Leonid Brezhnev?' she asked.

'There are others. Stay here . . .'

He got out and called loudly. Nobody answered. After some minutes he got back into the car exclaiming irritably that he wished he knew the language. He drove on slowly to the bend of the road so that the headlights gave him a view of other trees and bushes; and he did not see anything coming towards him. Around them the night was silent.

'Look,' he said, 'may I make a suggestion? As it's getting late I think we'd better turn round and go back the way we came. We'll meet someone back there, I'm sure.'

'I'd drive all night so long as we're together.'

'Sentimental fool,' he said affectionately, and turned the car.

Nearly halfway down the road he said: 'Stop, I think I saw someone over there.' He dowsed the lights and pulled up and got out calling to the darkness without gaining a response. As he did so he opened the rear door cautiously and lifted out the dead man. Still calling, he slung the body over his shoulder and only just managed to prevent her attempt to shut the door, and walked down the road. What remained of Zakharov proved heavier than he had expected, but at present he had worse problems on his mind. These were moments of extreme risk. Even if she did not drive away she could use his absence to report over the car bugs. He wished he had stayed home.

Some sixty yards from the car he dropped the body face down on the road. He bent to spread the legs and felt under the body to be sure the jacket was undone, got the gun from his pocket and wiped it carefully with his handkerchief, and put it into the right-hand pocket, and finally drew the arms straight down alongside the body. He turned the dead face away from the side of the road. It was the best fake he could manage in the circumstances.

'So long, mate,' he muttered. 'I'll apologize when we meet over there. And how do you feel now if there is an over there after all?'

He straightened and walked quickly back. Everything was so quiet it almost scared his butterflies. Perhaps the Fates intended him to believe he would get away with it and then—bingo! he'd've bought the lot. As he got near the car he started to laugh. Both doors were still open, he noted. She had comprehended his reason for playing it carefully. He felt inclined to pray.

'No good,' he said gustily between his laughter as he got in. 'He didn't understand me and the woman with him was nervous. Do I look violent?'

While he laughed he contrived to shut both doors simultaneously so that their clicks sounded as one. Irina joined in his laughter. It sounded spontaneous, the happiness of a woman at ease with her companion. She let it trail off as he put the car in gear and switched on the headlights.

Instantly the prone body leapt into view. As the car went forward he had an odd conviction that at any second Zakharov would spring to his feet like those Russian acrobats pretending to be soldiers. He listened to the night, manoeuvring the car while he did so.

'Phil honey, we certainly meet strange people,' she commented lazily. ' 'Member that man who got into our lift in Berlin?'

He hoped the words were intended to indicate cooperation.

'Whatever put him into your mind? I won't forget him. Wasn't he stoned? But I owe him a debt. If he hadn't tried to get fresh with you. I'd never have had the courage to kiss you.'

'Oh, I'd already intended you should.'

At that instant the near side front wheel struck Zakharov's head. Due to lack of time for rehearsal, the blow was heavier than he had intended and probably severed the dead man's spine. It also caused the car to rock sharply. It probably jarred the bugs sufficient to cause a momentary blur. Irina appeared to cover it instinctively though he did not wholly trust her seeming assistance at present.

'That was naughty,' she told him reprovingly. 'Be good and keep your hands to yourself or I shall do worse than hit the curb.'

'Then say you'll come,' he said, and watched the rear-view mirror without seeing any lights.

'I'll think about it. If you're good. I just can't bear to be mauled in an auto.'

'At this hour they're only bedrooms on wheels.'

'How horrible!'

He drove back across the river. In sight of the Foreign Affairs building he detoured down Smolensky Boulevard and on to where Krymsky Bridge crossed the river. At his suggestion they got out to admire the view. He saw no indication of any car following them.

When they halted to watch the treacly black swell of the river oozing past he felt her quivering. He put his arm round her and she rested heavily against him. It could well be a reaction to events though she had become a very good actress. Every lead he gave had been taken faultlessly and her responses were ingenious by their very simplicity. Beyond any doubt she could be a very dangerous woman. He felt a bit exposed.

For some moments she trembled violently. Her whole body shook and she had trouble with breathing. It could be a genuine attack of nervous reaction to events or an attempt to gain mastery over his natural defences as an agent, which she knew he would possess. When she got control of herself she remained silent for long minutes. Then she turned to him. Her first words showed she comprehended at least some of his thoughts.

'Trust me,' she entreated harshly. 'I am not frightened or weak. This is an ordinary reaction to something I had not expected. You are always in control of yourself. Our Russian temperament needs release when a strain has passed. But that is only part of it. Whatever your doubts, trust me. I will not betray you.'

'You are and will be magnificent.'

Irina looked up into his face. He saw her eyes watching his, a taut smile on her lips. 'That is nothing,' she said in a grateful tone. 'There is worse. How shall I have the strength to leave you tonight? I need you. My body needs your body to subdue it and give it peace. Do you mind being told the fierceness of my want of you? I am a woman willing to tell her lover she needs him.'

'And he needs her.'

'We must go or they may be suspicious.'

'First,' he said, 'this.'

She fitted herself close.

As they went back to the car she said: 'Ask me to meet you tomorrow night.'

There were few people and fewer cars in sight when Irina drew up outside the hotel. Everything appeared so ordinary that his mind found it rather unreal. He had a feeling there must be someone near whom he had missed. As they went through their banal leavetakings he had an intense longing for wide open empty spaces.

'That's enough for tonight,' she said fondly.

'Not for me.'

'Men,' she said tolerantly and then, like a promise, she whispered: 'Darling, wait, wait, until tomorrow.'

He got out reluctantly. 'You'd better be on time or terrible things will happen to me,' he said, and stood watching as she drove off. Watching her car disappear he sniffed the warm dry air and wondered if it was the *sukhovyei,* the hot dry wind from Central Asia or whether it was wishful thinking. Several cars passed while he stood there regaining his own inner composure. There were a few single-decker red-and-white buses, only half full; their occupants were mainly young people, probably going home from some sports events. He did some deep breathing and became aware of a vague headache. 'We'll see,' he said to himself. Then he hitched an English smile onto his handsome face and turned into the hotel.

It almost surprized him that there was no rush of security officials. Tomorrow morning might be very different. Now, yes, he needed time to think about Strelnikov and Konuzin and Zakharov and, not least, his own recent companion. It would do him good to sit down and think for a couple of weeks. He knew he had to be wary of her. She had a way of doing things which he liked.

As he started to enter his room he heard Martha Conroy call out: 'Philip! I've been waiting up for you!'

It was a moment for splendid fortitude.

12

A conviction of being in some danger from women came into his mind as he prepared to face another day and persisted through his morning chores amid a tidal slap of voices and feet at the exhibition.

None of his attempts to dispel it succeeded.

There was reason. Or should it be said he had cause? He was so confused that he had lost all contact with his mental grammar.

Some years ago he had read Gerald Durrell's superb book *The Overloaded Ark*. Much earlier he had reached a general conclusion that his head was constructed of the same material. At the time there had been excellent cause for his belief. Now, within the space of a few short hours, the compartments between the timber were so overcrowded that it would not have surprised him greatly if the whole thing had sunk, unable to remain buoyant let alone on course.

At present in this alien city he knew himself to be in such a dicey position that he dared not become too serious about it. People like Leprechaun soon reported back if an ebullient salesman whose stand attracted much attention and who could look forward to dinner with an attractive woman became deflated and worried overnight, preoccupied and frowning at his thoughts. Nothing would gain their interest quicker than any sign of uneasiness; the only concerns which capitalist salesmen were supposed to suffer from were hangovers and wives who did not understand them. He had to keep his cool and let his lovely features indicate sublime confidence in everything. He found it hard, another penalty of keeping up with the Muscovite Joneses. Now his nerves sweated so profusely that he felt dropsical. But glances into the full-length mirror which was part of the stand's fittings reassured him. They gave no hint of the unresolved confusions churning inside his mind until it felt like the grandfather of all cement-mixers.

In the steady sunlight of a day which became steadily warmer hour after hour they grew more intricate than they had seemed in the darkness of last night.

Once again he had to get his priorities right. It would help if some brilliant insight could provide him with a faultless sequence of events ahead and show how he could dash blithely through them.

Basically it was simple.

He had to get himself and his information home to Britain without endangering these other Britons on this stand beside him. It meant he had to get the microfilmed information from Strelnikov and find out about Irina and Konuzin. It meant he had to stay clear of investigations into what caused the death of Zakharov.

Simple.

Of course.

While the morning wore on an unwelcome new thought kept recurring to him. Irina and Zakharov had both recognized him faultlessly. There was bound to be a third. There always was a third. Or was that a lingering whiff of superstitions he had acquired during his flirtation with the theatre? Off-hand, he could think of several Russians whose memories just might be aroused if they saw him, individuals who had been accredited to various embassies and consulates and trade missions in the Middle East. It was just possible though he had only met each of them on two or three occasions and then briefly. Irina and Zakharov were different. Both of them had cause to remember him or, to be more precise, not to forget him. Quite possibly there were others who would remember him if he became linked with the death of Zakharov.

He could almost feel himself waiting for the bullet in the back of the head. Logic argued they would not execute him. Right now he would place no bets on that. Without having any guilt complexes about either, he had killed Gerin and been at least partly responsible for the death of Zakharov last night; no forensic scientist here would prove him innocent of the latter event, even though it was accidental. On the other hand, it might just suit Russian purposes to keep another British agent on ice after the usual hooha trial and international publicity in readiness for exchange with another Russian agent taken captive on some future occasion in Britain. It depended on how they interpreted the deaths of Irina's husband and Zakharov. Gerin and he had both been armed and Gerin was unlucky in fair duel. Zakharov's death would come under the heading of manslaughter. But the KGB had no record of having ever weakened to use what Russians called *spravedlivost,* fairness in the sense of justice. One of its members, or a whole team, might kill him while he resisted arrest as they put it. As he thought about it, that seemed the likeliest possibility.

'Wake up, old man,' he heard Keene say jovially. 'We are due to have another official party soon.'

'I had a short night.'

'Yes, I saw her. Super, as they say. That figure, those gorgeous legs, a real woman! I don't wonder you've been half-asleep since breakfast.'

'You have a dirty mind. I have a romantic heart.'

Keene tck-tcked worriedly. 'Watch it,' he warned, 'watch it. These women always play the romantic type for suckers. It gives 'em the upper hand to feel precious, a feeling of power. Keep the wench in line, old man. My motto used to be give 'em a little of what they fancy and let 'em wait till you feel like it again. But never romance, dear God no. You watch it.'

'I'll do that thing.'

'Will you come and attend to the unromantic Mr. Yamshikov and his fraternal committee?'

Silk found this hearty masculinity a bit wearing.

Fortunately, though against his inclination, he had no further chance to brood until lunchtime. Official groups trotted up to the stand for a routine peer, each accompanied by its own interpreter. Their questions seldom varied but every one had to be answered as if it was shrewd and a sign of unique intelligence. Among his favourite interpreters was an enormous woman with a vast and riotous bosom only partly clad by a thin white cotton blouse whose neck was wide open to every cooling breeze and with good cause if her manner provided a true guide. She strode around the stand like a model for Earth Mother, her superbly triumphant hips surging like an angry sea, her legs twice the size of those of any footballer. Another was a compact little man who ran about as if some internal mechanism kept him on the go. He could not be less than sixty-five but looked as if he felled a mighty oak by hand-axe every morning before breakfast to achieve his gleam of health. He was another of those Russians who spoke English without any trace of accent.

When the parties tailed off Silk glanced at his watch and decided to have lunch.

He contrived to ensure none of his companions accompanied him. Martha Conroy was in no mood for any sort of lunch; although she looked healthy she claimed to be suffering from her over-indulgence at the party.

For a change he decided to eat at a *kafe* near the Spartak Stadium. It was proof of his inner tension as he walked through the illusory coolth of tree shade and along sunbright paths whose heat struck up at him that he expected a rush of security agents from behind the trees to surround him. His mood was all wrong. No innocent man let his nerves imagine such an event; an agent was always an innocent man when among those who chose to be his enemies. Nor was he reassured when the trees proved devoid of malice. It could mean only that Irina was having a harsh interview trying to explain how she came to witness and not prevent the death of another Russian KGB man at the hands of the man who shot Gerin. It could also mean they were considering their best method of handling him because she had been his companion. They would ask her many questions. Her answers would be of interest. He trusted her as much as he trusted a politician making an election speech.

On the two occasions he glanced back his extra shadow resembled an ex-Red Army type. This individual, one of Leprechaun's replacements, wandered along sucking his teeth in the disgruntled manner of a man who had undertaken worthier tasks. Throughout their stroll to the *kafe* the shadow kept a careful thirty yards behind him. Everything about him suggested the KGB still assumed this particular quarry was an ordinary businessman from a capitalist country, one of the hundreds who needed routine surveillance every year. Such treatment irritated him. He still had no means of telling whether their interest was routine or proved personal danger.

Nothing made it a memorable luncheon. He sat with other breathing and ticking-over humans who also masticated and swallowed the edible fare put in front of them. Food was his least concern at present. He even forgot what it was while he ate it. What he did remember were moments of contact with Irina. They meant little but they were more than merely pleasant; perhaps he had not expected her to be able to kindle such heat. You could never tell: it might all be part of KGB routine. Certainly she had ensured he was fully aware of her carnal being, those restless moist lips, the husky voice expressing delight and gratification, those firm breasts, the positive waist above thighs which braced hard against his, her clinging arms and hands which gathered female memories of muscles and shapes. Until Zakharov disturbed them, and later after they had got rid of his body, she had used every female wile to entice and entreat, claim in order to be claimed, to stimulate desire through curiosity and assurances of her own need. Her skill was undeniable. An

older man could easily fall victim.
He munched his tepid Russian-style salad.

Shortly before five thirty he left Sportivnaya Metro station and joined the crowd of people heading for Luzhniki.

Normally he would feel envious of Luzhniki's planned opportunities for almost every variety of sportertainment. It had a vast arena, a magnificent open swim-pool, a covered palace used for an ice rink, a score of gymnasiums and other facilities which flabby and unhealthy British politicians failed to provide for their athletes. But on this particular jaunt his sole concern was to ensure no one followed him from the time he left the exhibition up at Sokolniki by a side exit. On his journey here along the Metro which Noel Coward had once described with shattering accuracy as a series of ornate gentlemen's lavatories', he had visited three of the smaller and lugubrious sections actually designed for this purpose though their performance left something to be desired. In them he had acquired some slight outward changes which could not be termed true disguise though they did alter his appearance for anyone looking for him in a hurry.

As he emerged from the station most people around him were talking animatedly about an athletic event they were going to witness. Overwhelmingly they were under thirty. Their voices rose into the warm air like a tangle of audible tapes. Most of them spilled out down the broad avenue which led beneath the overpass to the sports centre. A few idled looking around, presumably for companions they expected to meet. All of them were clad in dark clothes and white shirts, the few women in printed cotton frocks. This was the communist version of bread and circuses; they had enough money to follow sport events, which helped them forget the endless inefficiency of their bureaucrats in providing enough money for a higher standard of living. By contrast with the average Western worker in his non-working clothes they were poorly, often shoddily attired. And none dared to strike. Their so-called trade union leaders were Kremlin pawns who did exactly what their bosses told them. Fear was a great persuader. Where Coms took power, trade union leaders were blown balloons and trade unionists had no right to protest or demand.

Silk played it on memory. He turned smartly left as if going to the hotel alongside the Metro but walked past it and turned up a left-hand path and slowed down as if he expected someone to join him. Idly he heeled round. No one had followed him. He turned and went slowly down another path.

Moments later he tagged himself onto a group of foreign visitors about to visit Novodevichy Convent. Their guide, a middleaged woman who resembled an awkwardly tied large parcel in her grey coat and skirt and black blouse, spoke to them in fluent German. He listened to her with increasing awe. Only a Russian could get into their voice the bright note which announced a building was part of the History Museum and then convey resigned disgust in adding it had originated as a centre of religion and finally romp into chauvinistic adulation of the essentially Russian aspects of its architecture. Her performance was a fine example of how the Kremlin practised the nationalism it urged others to abolish. Such frantic hypocrisy always astonished him. He wished he could spare more time to listen to the poor woman.

Nobody followed him into the cemetery.

When he had first seen this particular corner of Russia it had surprised him. He had gone there to see the grave of the theatrical director Stanislavsky. Around the old boy were such writers as Chekhov and Gogol, quantities of people whose talents had given richness to Russian artistic life in Czarist days, plus a quantity of Old Bolsheviks and wartime leaders. It was a heterogeneous corner.

He walked slowly. What had struck him as incongruous on his previous visits and did so again now was how a regime which prided itself on its atheism had never provided a worthy cemetery for its heroes, an acre free from the taints it ascribed to religion. Maybe this was part of its basic inadequacy. Old Bolsheviks and other top Coms were stuffed away among men and women inspired by deep religious faith, many of whom suffered persecution in their fight for a free expression of ideas, a thing the Kremlin also denied precisely because they had no alternative burial place to provide. It was inadequate and part of the fundamental hypocrisy.

Several people passed as he paused by the graveside of Scriabin, the mystic composer who wanted to have a keyboard to project coloured lights to interpret his final work *Promethesus: The Poem of Fire.* He also intended to compose a sort of hymn of praise to unite all men to a Holy Spirit and wanted to set it in India which he had intended to visit and for which purpose he purchased a sun-helmet in London. Instead he died of a carbuncle on the top lip that caused blood poisoning. It was one way of going.

As Silk went on the man who claimed to be Strelnikov fell into step beside him.

'Do cemeteries interest you?' Strelnikov asked as if continuing a discussion. He spoke English.

'They interest me like other places I shall not stay at,' Silk agreed. 'Heaven, the Sea of Tranquillity, the core of the earth.'

'You do not believe in having a grave?'

Strelnikov sounded quite shocked. His scar glowed in the early evening light. A hint of strain showed on his face. This evening he wore a faded open-necked blue sports shirt, old grey trousers, well-worn imported brown sandals, and carried an ancient grey jacket over his arm. His hair had been done in another style, given a pains-taking parting with the front portion riased in a high quiff above his forehead. It lent him the appearance of an industrial worker with a fetish about physical fitness. In this city of close on seven million people it would have been sufficient disguise if it had not been for the scar.

With the scar . . . well, other men had them, not all like this one, but perhaps some bore similar scars. If he was Strelnikov, then he had the courage and recklessness of a man of true ideals, the lone fighter for a belief who deserved aid, one of those individuals, men and women, whose solitary walk through endless peril, whether in the hot days of World War Two or these days of the cold war, put the noise and violence of crowds of excitement-seeking students to shame. If he was not Strelnikov there would be moments of breath-holding soon.

'I prefer the Hindu exit for myself,' Silk said. 'How are you?'

'Very well. It has been a glorious day.'

'Yes.'

They fell silent as a young couple came towards them hand in hand. If appearances were a true guide the man was about twenty and the girl no more than eighteen. Their dreamy absorption in each other had the atmosphere of nineteenth-century romanticism and was charming. It was also very Russian.

Directly they had gone out of earshot the man whom Silk had to hope was Strelnikov put his hand into a pocket of his jacket.

Silk went two paces aside. In this age of powerful tiny bugs conversations could be clearly heard over considerable distances. His only slight hope of not being overheard was to be out of range. It would be difficult.

'How have things been with you?' he asked quietly.

'Our situation is deteriorating rapidly,' Strelnikov answered harshly. 'Two or three cosmonauts circling the earth are no proof of progress in agricultural production and the supply of consumer goods. You probably know there is a power struggle in the Kremlin because of the failure of our agricultural policies and industrial output. There is also another struggle going on between moderates who have Czechoslovakia on their conscience and those who want to return to the even harder lines of Stalinism. Our Russia is slipping back into its Stalinist copy of

Czarism. Everyone in the Kremlin wants to wear the Shapka Monomakha. Our people suffer needlessly. We are inefficient and our children are educated only to do what the politicians want.'

Silk thought it a good beginning but decided his one neck required further safeguards. 'Did you say the Shapka Monomakha? he asked.

'Have you never heard the favourite legend of our Czars? It has influenced our attitude for nearly a thousand years. According to the usual version a Prince of Kiev, Vladimir Monomakh, sent part of his army to wage war on Constantine Monomachus in Constantinople. Constantine sent the Greek Metropolitan to Kiev with presents and his own crown to offer peace between all Orthodox nations under the joint sovereignty of himself and that of the 'Great Rus' Vladimir. Our Vladimir was not a humble man.'

Silk kept silent.

'He had himself crowned with Constantine's crown, the Shapka Monomakha, the cap of Monomachus, and announced himself to be the divinely ordained Czar of all Russia. Five hundred years later a council of the Church proclaimed that in power and position our Czars were like 'the highest God'. As you will agree, the disease is contagious. Our present leaders believe they are destined to be rulers of all Russians and other peoples. They are simple men, vastly impressed by their own power. It is their conviction that Russia is destined to rule the earth. They too believe themselves, as their actions prove, to be like 'the highest God'.

'Not by divine right.'

'Ah, such sadness for them,' Strelnikov said sadly. 'Some of our leaders want to revive belief in God so they can claim our revolution and Central Committee were appointed by Him.' He shook with silent laughter. 'It may happen in another thirty years. What celebrations! Fireworks. A holy war to claim the Middle East. A man and a woman crash landing on a planet to claim it for Russia and start the first Earth migrant family. Such celebrations!'

Silk smiled. 'That sounds like the sort of joke an underground *Krokodil* would print,' he commented.

'They are in an awkward position,' Strelnikov said. 'They believe their political beliefs to be the only true solution to how a state can be conducted but they have denied themselves any claim that their beliefs are divinely inspired and with such beliefs guiding them the country is more inefficient than most capitalist countries. Consequently their main aims now are to cause capitalist countries to become chaotic through anarchy spread by their agents provocateurs. These men are not agents provocateurs in the true sense, you understand, but their intentions are similar.'

Neither of them spoke as a group of tourists padded busily past them. As the tourists passed they turned down another path. Silk glanced round to ensure no one was near enough to overhear them. He felt a certain amount of relief at how Strelnikov expressed himself, his criticisms of the Kremlinites being harsher, often more venomous, than was necessary if this was a trap. But he was still a long way from home.

'We hear things are not happy inside the Kremlin,' he said.

'They never have been and never will be,' Strelnikov affirmed. 'How can such a system of politics permit ordinary government to be conducted? Ever since Lenin died, and before then, there has been friction inside the Party. A certain aura attached to Stalin because he was one of the original conspirators who produced the revolution and then by deceit and trickery put the Bolsheviki in power. But he had feuds. According to his low mentality he had to have Trotsky assassinated. But by the very act of assassination he caused Trotsky to become a martyr, for it was Trotsky who masterminded the actual revolution. But Trotsky was only one of Stalin's victims. There were many more. You know them. Everyone knows them. And since Stalin died, whether naturally or because he was poisoned as some say, there has been nothing but intrigue to gain ultimate power. Not to improve life for the people but to claim that life for them must be better now because a new man has finally seized power to gratify his lust to dominate.'

Strelnikov seemed to realize that Silk was picking his brains to gain insight into the present position here. His answers, his flow of words, suggested he had done a considerable amount of thinking through and around the politics of his country. Silk felt himself warming to the man. On the assumption that Strelnikov was expressing his opinion, then obviously he would not do so if he thought his fellow-countrymen were well served by and had a chance of good government from the present system of government.

He remained silent while a posy of chattery schoolgirls broke loose around them and reformed behind them.

'You think it will continue?' he said.

'What else? There is no revolutionary aura to protect another Stalin. Brezhnev and Kosygin will not last much longer. We may have a reversion to a Stalinist type of government in order to temporarily still criticisms of government, but it will not last. It cannot last. Any new Stalin must improve the material conditions of the people, because we have lost the space race with America, or he will die mysteriously. But there will be no revolution here. Our system of government cannot be overthrown unless there is world war.'

Silk decided to take a risk. 'I see what you mean,' he commented. 'I forgot to mention that I know a cousin of yours. Viktor Primakov.'

'Poor Viktor! There is a case in point. Look what happened to him as a result of loyalty to the men in the Kremlin. Death and disgrace.'

'He told me several things about your shared experiences when you were boys.'

Strelnikov smiled. 'Those were good days,' he said. 'What a tragedy it is that children grow up to be men and women.'

In the next ten minutes Silk became reasonably sure that the man beside him was Strelnikov. No one could remember such incidents as the man recalled at the drop of a hat. Several incidents were identical to what Primakov had told him during days when they had pottered about Inner Mongolia beset by Chinese troops. Nothing in any briefing could have prepared Strelnikov to have such memories revived by a stranger.

He cut into another anecdote. 'What happened to Primakova?' he asked.

'Poor woman, she is here in Moscow.'

'Alone?'

'She married a Party official last winter.'

'Do you know him?'

'We have met. His name is Leonid Polikarpov. He works in the Ministry of Foreign Affairs.'

'An unimportant post?'

'No. He is highly placed, a key man in the Chinese Bureau.'

Silk thought for a moment. Then he said: 'Primakov will be interested to hear it.'

Strelnikov spoke half a dozen sentences before he became aware of what Silk had said. He stopped to look at a tombstone. 'What did you say?' he asked, and when Silk repeated it he asked abruptly: 'What do you mean?'

Silk glanced around to ensure no one overheard them. Silently he held out his hand for the films. Frowning, Strelnikov handed them over without a word. Silk was aware of a demo of cowardly butterflies, on whom he could always rely, as he pocketed them. He gave the Russian fresh packets of cassettes for the powerful little Minox cameras. Strelnikov put them away into the pockets of his jacket. His face had gone stiff.

'You are telling me he is alive, my cousin? he asked.

'There is reason to believe so.'

'Where is he? What is he doing?'

'I have not seen him for nearly a year.'

Strelnikov stared at him. 'God!' he exclaimed gently. 'You saw him a year ago. He is not dead?'

'He was not dead then. He was alive in China.'

'China!'

'We decided not to stay,' Silk assured him. 'Neither of us was there from choice. He had been sent there. I arrived accidentally. He will be interested to know Tamara married Polikarpov. It distressed him that she accepted the Party rule to let him die to suit its aims. He realized then she never had any love for him. He worshipped her. He talked about her endlessly.'

'My God!' Strelnikov whispered. 'That female camel! My poor Viktor! He loves her still?'

'He remembered her with intense clarity.'

'He would. We Russians suffer if we love. He was a romantic.'

'Your last Czar suffered too,' Silk commented.

'True. It either made him weak or brought out a weakness in him.'

'Viktor talked about her as if he had only just left her.'

Strelnikov shook his head. 'My poor cousin,' he said in an unsteady voice. 'He is better rid of her.'

'I told him so.'

As they went on the Russian asked: 'When did you meet him?'

'While the Red Army was invading Czechoslovakia. It turned him into a bitterly unhappy man.'

'All true Russians know it was an event of national shame which they will never live down. None of them now respect the men in the Kremlin.'

They walked in silence for some minutes. Silk had a feeling that Strelnikov was absorbing the shock of learning that his officially dead cousin was alive. After all the publicity hooha over a substituted corpse of unknown origin, one of those emotion-choked occasions beloved of Com Agitprop organizers, full of tearful rhetoric, sad flags, proud banners, the bereft relict's cascading tears of unbearable loss, weepy-eyed distinguished pallbearers on their comradely trudge over the salt of their misery, fine publicity hocus-pocus to impress the mentally retarded who loved a 'big funeral', it must be a shock to the man to learn that Primakov was only another official corpse. He let Strelnikov alone to get over it. They paced down another path.

At length Strelnikov raised his head. Undoubtedly he was shocked. No one could fake the expression on his face.

'I should have realised. They have done it to others. Primakova refused to meet me after the funeral. There were other signs. At the time I overlooked them.'

'It happens to everyone.'

Strelnikov nodded. 'Thank you for trusting me,' he said gratefully. 'You have taken a risk in speaking so candidly.'

'Both of us take risks. It is harder for you.'

'I think not. It cannot be easy for a man to run such risks when your politicians are so . . . what is your word? Irresolute?'

'Every country has its unsure years. We'll get out of ours. I think I should tell you that your cousin works for what he believes will be a better world of his own free will. No one has or will threaten him.'

Strelnikov nodded. They were silent as a group of people came towards them, two greying men followed by their wives, the sort of people who always visited famous interment yards. When they passed out of hearing Strelnikov drew a deep breath and looked up at the cloudless sky. Much of the tension had gone out of his face. He looked younger and quixotically more confident than at any previous moment. Silk searched his mind for something to give the change of expression life in his mind, and realised that the Russian looked like a youth confident of his rightness and unafraid of dangers which he knew existed around him.

'There is much I would like to discuss with you,' he said, almost regretfully. 'It is good to talk without heed of what one says. How we endure our silence, God knows.

Next time, yes? Now we must not be too long though I wish we could talk until tomorrow.'

'Next time.'

'Yes,' Strelnikov said with relief. 'We shall be easier with each other then. Now I must tell you things because I have been unable to photograph some documents.'

'Go ahead.'

'You know that while Stalin was alive the Kremlin believed every war helped them to extend the area of their type of communism. They cannot foment large wars now. Their main aim at present is to weaken every country internally by every available means of insecurity and mass dissention, to cause a breakdown of the social order which can be turned into revolution. Supposed anarchist disorders, trade union lawlessness, race riots, economic instability which can cause student and hippie violence, small wars anywhere to give those hypocrites in the Kremlin a chance to pose as peacemakers and sell arms. The warmongers! Anything which will undermine capitalism and conceal their own failures.

'It must take a large organisation.'

'Many men and women sacrifice their youth and comfort,' Strelnikov told him. 'Our rulers want the world. They may make a temporary deal with Peking in order to try to gain it. Our masters are megalomaniacs, like some of your trade union leaders, yes? They believe themselves to be infallible. They disgrace our Russia, they betray the ideals of the revolution, but no one here will stop them. People prefer safety to truth.'

'What about your intelligents?' Silk asked using the Russian word for intelligentsia.

'They fought bravely during the era of Khrushchov and immediately afterwards. Now their cry for truth and justice has ended exactly like the Hundred Flowers period which Mao allowed the Chinese for a little while. Both governments ended it for the same reason. To keep themselves in power. Your communists too would deny people free speech and prevent honest criticism. Consequently our agriculture and industry are always backward.'

Silk let the other man talk on. One of his thoughts concerned the reference to the true ideals of the revolution. Their betrayal began when Lenin and his associates found a device to keep control of former Czarist colonies and perpetuate Russian imperialism under another name.

As they went on Strelnikov talked fluently about the Kremlin's intended naval strategy in the Mediterranean, along north African coasts. At one point he added: 'I have included details of where subs are scheduled to go around Britain for the next few years, from Scapa Flow to Portland, and down the eastern seaboard of the U.S. You probably know KGB agents land from subs on your coasts at night with money for disaffectionist groups. Ah, I nearly forgot, there is so much . . . the Kremlin hopes, if plans are made to reopen the Suez Canal, to have its 'experts' stationed there to supervize repairs and then control it. They need it opened to get submarines quickly into the Indian Ocean.'

Later he said: 'Does the West know they are still arresting naval officers and shooting them without trial for complicity in the plot at Tallin?'

'We've heard rumours. Go on.'

Half an hour later they halted near the entrance. No one was near.

'I hope you will be the next courier,' Strelnikov said as they shook hands. 'Remember me to Viktor if you see him.'

'Have you any message for him?'

'I am overjoyed he is alive and wish him well whatever he does.'

'He shall be told if I can locate him.'

Strelnikov smiled. *'Chastlyvo!'* he said.

'So long.'

Strelnikov swung away and went off. Silk followed at a slower pace.

Outside the main entrance to the convent grounds Silk

paused, glancing round as if uncertain of which direction to take. He caught sight of Strelnikov striding away through sauntering groups of people, a sturdy athletic figure who looked even lonelier now precisely because nothing about him appeared lonely, more vulnerable because he seemed so assured. He turned the corner, jacket over arm, faded blue shirt illuminated by sunlight as he strode free of shadow, and then he vanished from sight.

Silk made his way towards the Metro. It was just on seven o'clock. Now all his hours ahead were going to be full of tensions. His unwilling nerves would have to carry him through every minute until he reached London airport.

As he climbed into the first subway train he could have used some of those unfree national health pills dished out back home. He could have sworn he saw Leprechaun getting into the next coach. His knees felt weak.

13

He finished the return journey via the Metro without incident but knowing that the next five days would be among the longest in his life if he was alive at the end of them. Five whole days. He licked lips gone dry at the thought. One hundred hours of waiting to get these cassettes of film to safety. Plus whatever time it would take the airplane to reach Heathrow and provided he was on it.

As he left the Metro station he tried to count his blessings. At least he was back on the schedule which he and Priest had arranged prior to his departure from London. In many ways his easiest hours would come after the exhibition closed and he had seen off his innocent companions. He preferred being alone, certainly without a feeling of responsibility for those ignorant of his real task. Alone he could take risks to protect himself or try to run for it. At present though his problems seemed to outweigh his blessings. There were the cassettes to try to conceal from any deliberately or casually searching eye. He had to expect some build-up of tension inside himself and anticipate its various forms. Not least of his problems was the question posed by Irina. She was an unstable factor, impossible to take for granted in any capacity. Everyone knew the KGB used women more effectively than the Japanese had used them prior to World War Two. Zakharov might also become a major worry. That depended in part on Irina. He corrected himself; in large part. Worse of all though would be the waiting. Five days. One hundred hours plus. It appalled him. He was not equipped to demonstrate such phenomenal patience.

He went up to his room feeling a vast weight on his shoulders.

Promptly at eight o'clock Irina came swiftly across the hotel lobby to where he sat leafing through a four months' old copy of *Paris Match*.

By every standard she really did look pretty good. As he stood up to greet her he thought the plain white microskirted cotton frock a perfect foil for her darkly suntanned neck and arms. Her black hair was piled on top of her head to leave her neck cool. An unmistakable brightness warmed her pale eyes as she came towards him. She appeared completely confident, a sign which had his suspicions poised like greyhounds ready to go. Incongruously she might be any woman reasonably free from stress arriving to spend an evening with her lover; she even looked like a sigh of relief as she came to him. It warned him.

'Phil darling, do I look all right, am I late?' she asked and held out both hands, her face raised. As he kissed her proferred cheek her left hand slid a small folded slip of paper into his. She drew back but not before his nose told him she was using a piquant French perfume.

'You look–what is the Russian word for delicious?

Vkusnil?'

'Who cares? Just so you like me.'

' "Like" is small potatoes. You look gorgeous and you are on time.'

He saw a sultry-eyed Egyptian gazing at him with sulky envy. Every hair of the Nassah moustache bristled. Both its owner and he were aware that Irina wore very little under the white frock.

'One of my colleagues is quite right,' he said, and put his hands into his pockets. 'He noticed you have superb legs.'

Her smile deepened. 'They are strong,' she said gently, and laughed suddenly as if she wanted to laugh without having a social reason for doing so, the way some children still laugh. 'I've been rushed off the ordinary feet attached to these superb legs–do you share his opinion . . .'

'Oh, his description is just a pallid imitation of my thoughts.'

'Gee, aren't you an old smoothie?' she said pleasedly. '–interviewing agents if you follow me.'

'Willingly, any old where or hour.'

'It's been too wonderful to bother. Their summer here is surely drier than the humid swelter we get back in New York. This one certainly is.'

'A splendid day. A quiet warm evening. An exciting and lovely woman. What more could a man want? Or her? Would you like a drink?'

'Would you?'

'I'm easy.'

She nodded. 'I'd sooner wait,' she decided. 'Where shall we go?'

'You know this town better than I do. Some restaurant where we feed today, not tomorrow, and there are no flowers interrupting my view of your face. Do you feel scorched? Half a dozen chaps here are about to kidnap you. Look the other way, at the Egyptian.'

A glint seemed to rise in her extraordinary eyes. No, it should be the other way round. It was like seeing a gleam of sunlight penetrate deep water. He had seen it when he had been skin-diving in the Caribbean. She moistened the corners of her lips.

'Do you think I bother about other men?' she asked quietly. 'I want you to be excited and content with what they will never have and has been yours for a long time.'

'They can see how I feel.'

Evidently the reply satisfied her.

'There is a place in Ulitsa Gorkogo which specializes in Azerbaijan food.'

He smiled. Trust a woman to recall a detail to suggest binding intimacy. They had first met among the spry centenarians of Azerbaijan.

'You obviously want me to stay alive a long time.'

'Phil honey, a long time will be just too short.'

As they left the hotel her arm kept his hand pressed against her waist.

While she drove them to a parking space close to the restaurant he read the note she had given him. It said the police believed Zakharov had been killed by a hit-and-run driver but because he worked for the KGB they had to investigate other possible causes. It added that she had permission to take him for a drive outside the city streets after dinner if he wished it. He used his lighter to burn the paper carefully and then tossed the dissolving ash out of the window.

'Have you got to work tonight?' she asked.

'There's always book work. What the heck? It can wait.'

'What shall we do?'

'You choose.'

'A movie.'

'Okay.'

'Would you like some fresh air? I guess the hall got hot today.'

'I sure reckoned I'd gotten me a personal sweat-box.'

She laughed. 'Your Yankee accent wouldn't fool anyone,' she told him in a fond tone. 'Fresh air it is.'

He only hoped everyone back home knew the risks he took for them.

Throughout dinner he sensed a barely suppressed excitement in Irina. He did not need to look at her to be conscious of it. Although it was a high-falutin' simile it reminded him of the brooding electric sensation you detect quivering in the desert air, up in Khorosan, down in the Empty Quarter, twenty four hours ahead of those great booming storms which rage for hours over the sand and rock. A fanciful comparison, sure, but not without cause. Her hands were restless too. She ate as if she had not eaten for a week. For a liqueur they had a fiery Armenian cognac which had no effect on her, proof that she was too tense to relax. And every so often she invented means to remind him how she relied on his resolution to get both of them out of the country. Her very tension kept him relaxed.

'Where shall we go?' she asked as they left the restaurant.

'Would it break any rules if we went south?'

'We can always apologize and show we've got no camera.'

'Yes,' he agreed, and felt the films weighing down his pockets. He would not have been astonished if they caught fire. But he had found no safe place to leave them at the hotel. He hoped to God they didn't fall foul of any promotion-seeking *politsyoiskyoi.*

They drove out through the usual evening confusion of trucks spewing thick black evil-smelling exhaust fumes, a smaller quantity of cars and taxis, a headlong rush of pedestrians across wide streets, and were soon heading past the incongruous mixture of high-rise blocks of flats and houses like hovels. Quantities of angry dogs prowled along some poorer streets, scavenging in heaps of suburban litter.

It did not take them long to reach the city limit at the junction of the circumferential motorway at the Warsaw Highway clover-leaf. Almost at once they were in the wide forest belt.

Here the traffic was definitely sparse. It consisted of a few long-distance lorries and small clusters of teenage cyclists pedalling idly along through shadow-broken light from the westering sun, and the odd tourist coach. Most trees were conifers, larch and pine, though there were quantities of birch, the tree associated with Moscow. Large clouds of midges hung in the air and the heat had a distinct sultriness, the moist heaviness of summers recalled in scores of wistful novels written in exile by White Russians. They passed a few isolated *dachas,* villas, mainly broken down and seemingly relicts from earlier days. He would have liked to see Nikulina Gora, the *dacha* settlement of the leading cultural luminaries, by all accounts a luxurious district full of the highest paid scientists, painters, dancers, poets, composers, writers, film players, musicians, and others of similar talents which they had sold to the Party in exchange for a quiet life. Most of them also maintained sumptuously appointed villas on the shores of the Black Sea, the Russian Cote d'Azur or Florida, from where they commuted by airplane to Moscow for work during the worst winter months. It was a largely ignored bit of hypocrisy, kept quiet not to enrage the workers in their dark clothes and monotonous days of just doing a job for food and rent.

No doubt someone had said: the aristocracy is dead, long live the aristocracy.

He almost said it out loud himself.

They drove past dirt roads which undoubtedly formed part of the spring *rasputitsa* when roads and lanes vanished under floods of rain and melted snow which formed a vast sloppy treacle of mud. These roads, straggling off into the trees, were proof that the Russians had not yet utilized the resources of a totalitarian government to rid themselves of problems which every wealthy nation should have solved in this technological age.

'Darling.'

'I know,' he said apologetically. 'I was admiring you, enjoying the scenery and air. It's marvellous to relax.'

'Do you like being taken for a ride?'

'You make it sound most attractive. Drive on.'

'Would you like a walk? I guess we can find somewhere.'

A coldness tightened round the base of his spine.

'Why do women always want exercise?' he complained. 'Yes, fine. You choose the place.'

Some twenty minutes later they stopped on a broad side-road quite a distance on the right of the main intercities road. Presumably it led round to other highways connected to the capital. He had a suspicion it also led to military areas. On either side were dense silver birch copses broken by other broadleaf deciduous trees and conifers. A familiar panic-demo started inside his stomach. An entire army could hide here. An additional complication was the sun, a fiery orange ball glittering ahead of them as it fell down the cloudless sky at a rate of knots. He always distrusted an atmosphere of rustic peace with enough birdsong to deafen everyone.

Irina put her hand on his. He saw the other gripped her bag tightly, a sight which could portend anything. 'You lead,' she said quietly.

They got out of the car and, hands linked, wandered on down the road.

Roughly three hundred yards farther on the road veered to the right. After another hundred yards it curved left and a rough narrow lane went off through thickets of birches. Irina did not question his decision to choose the lane. Her acquiescence meant nothing. Nor did this silence full of clamorous birdsong. No word came from her till they were out of sight of the road. Then she halted and tugged him round to face her.

'Search me,' she told him simply and put her bag down

at their feet.

He did so. There was nothing infernal secreted on her. As he nodded she gave a bitter smile and let his arms go round her. Unlike the previous evening, unlike her mood of only a short while ago, she was stiff and unyielding and silent. It took some effort on his part but finally the thaw set in. Almost immediately it did so she clung to him as if afraid her legs lacked the strength to support her.

She was in a rare mood for punishment. It went on and on like an endurance test. Her lips, her mouth, her tongue, the pressures of her body, did everything possible for a woman standing on her feet who wanted to persuade a man this contact was a substitute for true reality. It helped him keep control while he listened for a soft footstep which could mean a very nasty headache unless he acted swiftly. He knew he would hear only one or two, if any. While he went on listening she came up for air. Some of her tension had been replaced by another stress and her eyes had changed. Almostly furiously her clenched hands beat on his chest while she muttered some of the earthy endearments left out of Chekhov's plays. Angrily too she stooped to pick up and open her bag. She drew out a small though serviceable automatic and held it out to him.

'You will need this, my love,' she said. Her husky whisper suggested that she too suspected the woods were crawling with troops or police. 'If you believe we must fail, shoot me. I have no wish to be alive here. I will bring you the bullets for it when we go.'

Without answering he examined the weapon. Its name, stamped on the butt, meant nothing to him. Apparently it came from a Siberian factory. Its designer had based it on an older type of Berretta.

He gave it back to her. 'Show me how it works,' he said. 'I've never seen this make before.'

She nodded. With the bag slung over her shoulder, she released and slid out the empty clip, tested the firing mechanism, pointed out how the safety-catch was awkwardly placed for anyone who had a large hand, reinserted the clip and locked it inside. She held it out to him.

He took it and did everything she had done while he continued to expect the woodland around them to erupt and wiped it clean of fingerprints and memorized its details as it lay on the handkerchief spread over his open hand.

'Neat,' he said appreciatively and brought her bag round and opened it and put the automatic back inside and closed the bag. 'No.'

'Dorian.'

'No. We'll drop it in the river when we get back.'

'Listen to me.'

'Listen to me,' he told her. 'You say you want to leave here. Many people, do men and women less intelligent and more intelligent than both of us. You haven't told me what plan you have to leave here with me. All right, we'll discuss it in a moment. But if it should fail and we were found to have weapons I might be gaoled but you would be shot because you work for the KGB. You have another gun for yourself?'

'Yes,' she said sullenly. 'We shall not fail. If we do, it will not matter whether I have a gun or not. They will shoot me!'

'Do you usually have one when you go abroad?'

'I never go alone. It is not permitted. A man comes with me. He gives me a gun if I have to do something alone.'

'Where is it?'

'At my hotel. They keep it and I get it for shooting practice.'

'Where is it kept?'

'I return it to the manager, an old KGB man.'

'Do you practice regularly?'

'Usually, unless I am too busy.'

'So if you asked for it on a day when you wouldn't normally practice it might attract attention?'

At length, grudgingly, she conceded: 'Yes.' She had

averted her eyes while he questioned her. A nerve flickered at the corners of her lips as if she found it an effort to control herself.

He had not finished.

'There were no scratches on this gun. It looks factory-fresh. Where did you get it?'

She lowered her face. 'There is a black market in guns,' she answered. 'People go in for *spekulatsiya,* black marketeering. It has increased again since we invaded Czechoslovakia. Workers at factories which produce them steal most of them but others are stolen in transit.'

'Does the government do anything about it?'

'Sometimes the security forces uncover a gang of thieves or just one man. They are always executed.'

He thought for a moment. 'Is it possible,' he began slowly, 'that some guns go onto the black market to discover who buys them illegally?'

'It is possible,' she agreed unwillingly.

'How long ago did you get it?'

'. . . more than a year . . . fourteen months.'

'Here? In Moscow?'

'No, I was in Vladivostok. Many workers there are dishonest. They are Asians. They steal anything. They sell it to Koreans or Chinese or Japanese sailors. It goes on all the year round. Our government keeps silent about it because it wants to believe theft is due to capitalism and cannot happen in communist countries unless the thief is insane or a traitor.'

She sounded evasive, confident only when talking about something impersonal.

After a pause he said: 'Irina, if we don't trust each other we won't stand a change of success. Suppose you tell me the truth about how you got it?'

They went through another period of indecision. Like a schoolgirl she watched one shoe scuff the dusty ground. Then she gave an exasperated sigh. 'We were working on another case,' she told him reluctantly, 'to do with Chinese agents. Peking is determined to regain control of the whole area Vladivostok and the country north is full of its agents. One afternoon we raided a house to arrest men and women holding a Maoist meeting to claim that the whole of eastern Siberia belongs historically to China. After we had taken them away I found a cache of automatics hidden in a cellar. I took one,' she said defiantly, and ended on a worried note: 'I did not want you to know I am a thief.'

He tipped up her face and kept fingers under her chin until her uneasy gaze met his. 'You're determined to go, aren't you?' he commented. 'So why take needless risks? You'll only worsen things for yourself if you get found out before you actually start. Don't tell me any more lies or we may run straight into other problems.' He stared at her. 'Will you promise?'

'It is hard, I am used to taking decisions for myself . . . yes, I promise.'

He nodded and took her elbow in his hand and turned her back down the road. 'We'd better get started or they'll wonder what has happened to you,' he said as they started to retrace their steps. He glanced round at the trees. Nothing stirred in his sight. 'How did you intend we should get away?'

'Do you mean it?' Irina asked unsurely.

'Well, we'll have to find a way. Go on, tell me.'

Each detail proved it to be a typically Russian scheme.

As they wandered slowly back she told him how just over three years ago a married British woman named Mary Fraser, who had run off from her husband and two children to be with her Turkish Cypriot waiter lover, had sold her passport to a Russian agent in Istanbul. Several weeks later it reached Moscow among a number of others to be filed away among the thousands which had accumulated over the years—British, American, Canadian, South American, Scandinavian, French, West German, Dutch, Italian, Spanish—and were carefully kept for future use by KGB agents. Irina had discovered Mary Fraser's passport nearly a year later while she was working in KGB Records. She had noticed that Mrs Fraser bore a distinct photographic resemblance to herself. Intrigued, she had taken the passport to the files to find out what information they had on the woman. There was nothing. By some chance the Fraser passport was among the handful which vanished into the cabinet without being recorded.

'Does it happen often?' Silk interrupted.

'No system is perfect. A lot of people are willing to sell their passport if they want to disappear. They are well paid. One official told me they probably mislay five or six a year, sometimes more. It happens in cycles, usually when someone new takes over or some event makes them careless.'

Impulse had prompted her to keep the passport. She soon realized that basically it was more than impulse. Like others, she had been critical of the trial of the two writers Yuri Daniel and Andrei Sinyavsky for writing short stories which criticized aspects of life in the USSR and she had been shocked by the ostracism of Boris Pasternak for his novel *Doctor Zhivago* which she had read while out of Russia on a mission. She became disgusted with the men in the Kremlin for telling her to ostracize Daniel's wife Larissa, who had been her friend since they were children.

'It is like the Law of Suspects of the French Revolution!' she exclaimed bitterly. 'You remember it.'

' "Suspects are those who by their conduct, their connexions, their remarks, or their writings show themselves to be partisans of tyranny." If my memory is correct. Another of the dictatorial methods of saying, who is not with us is against us.'

'Yes,' she said, and drew a deep breath. 'It is so good to talk freely to a man without fear of his running to someone to report any casual word.'

When more and more of the intelligents escaped to the West she had begun to question the life of those who allowed the Kremlin to dictate their every thought Soon afterwards Svetlana Alliluyeva escaped: the daughter of

Stalin himself fled to the West! one woman able to defy and outwit the entire KGB! Moscow had scarcely recovered from the shock when heavy Russian tanks rolled across the border into Czechoslovakia and within weeks the threat to Romania was being mounted. Another literary storm had burst upon the capital when its people heard that Alexander Solzhenitsyn was being disgraced; by then everyone knew the Kremlin, and its well-fed puppets in the Writers' Union, were being forced to condemn Solzhenitsyn because he too had criticized the Stalinist regime. Now the pressure was on others. Everyone was watching because the literary scene suddenly meant more than it had for years; it had become an arena, ideas forcing the Kremlin to show its repressive and autocratic dictatorship. People knew that men like the Academician Sakharov, a nuclear physicist, and Andrei Amalrik, were in danger of arrest and imprisonment in Siberia. Just as in Czarist days.

'No one shall dictate how I think,' Irina said angrily. 'Those men in the Kremlin imagine they rule unintelligent peasants. If we are uneducated, whose fault is it? They have had power for over fifty years. If we are still peasants, not highly trained industrial workers, who is to blame? Those of my generation are their children. Western Europe has recovered from World War Two. Russian industry and agriculture are still inefficient, still suffering from shortages. Why did we incur such fatalities when we fought the Nazis? Because Stalin and his men were inefficient, more concerned with their palace intrigues, in playing little Czars, than in lifting Russia into the modern age. All the Party chiefs are like the old Czarist aristos, kissing each other while they wait to kill each other. They are the new *boyarin,* the aristocracy. They sit in their *Duma,* which they call the party praesidium, and decide who shall be the *luchshie lyudi,* the best people. And the *luchshie lyudi* are always those with the longest warmest tongues for licking. But Russia is still last among the nations in giving the people a better life.'

She sounded extremely bitter.

'They have done a lot of space exploration,' he reminded her.

'What good does it do ordinary people to be kings of an infinite wasteland in which they cannot grow cabbages?'

'What about Southeast Asia? It can be said the West has failed there.'

She shrugged. 'Kremlin policy in Southeast Asia and Africa and the Middle East and South America is dominated by two things,' she said. 'One, it must seek to prevent the spread of Maoism among the peasants. Two, it must continue its plan to destroy capitalism. It can only prove communism right by destroying whatever is more efficient than itself. It has no plan to better the peoples of those countries, only to destroy their present political systems. It will give anyone arms and let them be killed in order to serve the masters of the Kremlin whatever their names.' She shrugged again. 'So far as Southeast Asia is concerned, particularly Vietnam, the Kremlin has blocked every international attempt to get the combatants to declare an armistice and discuss their dispute. It will always prevent discussion unless it suits its long-term plan of world domination.' A frown creased her forehead. 'Why do we talk politics when we have to enjoy this evening and each other? I only want to talk about us. I want to hear nonsense from you and tell you how I love and admire you.'

He let it go. 'There will be time,' he said. 'Tell me about your plan.'

Irina simmered for a few moments. Suddenly she smiled and pulled his arm round her waist and held it there. 'You are right,' she agreed with an abrupt change of mood, and started to describe the background to her plan.

When she returned from Yemen after Gerin was killed her only foreign assignments had been to countries inside the Soviet bloc and West Germany. Escape from Russia had become her sole ambition. But she was a woman. On each foreign visit she was too carefully watched to be able to get away. She had come to believe her next visit to Germany might provide a fair chance. Within days she had heard he was coming to Moscow. She managed to keep the information to herself and tried to work out a plan to leave Russia with him. Then she had learned, again from Marie, that he was not coming. She had abandoned her plan. Out of curiosity she visited the exhibition. When she saw him she arranged with Pekelis to attend the party.

'Did you expect to recognize who had taken my place?' he asked.

'I hoped you would be there,' she replied with every sign of honesty. 'In our work, plans are often dropped and picked up within hours.'

He knew that to be true.

'So Marie got the information from Jeremy?'

'Yes.'

'How many other people know?'

'Nobody, my darling. Everything from her goes first through me. I am like a secretary who decides what is important in the morning mail. It has given me many opportunities.'

'Did the information Jeremy sent her pass through you too?'

'Yes.'

He forwent the temptation to press for knowledge of Jeremy's identity. It would be a psychological error at this stage.

'I see,' he said.

An edge of excitement sharpened her voice as she outlined her plan. She could alter Mary Fraser's passport without much trouble so that it appeared to belong to Mrs Mary Foot. It would not be dangerous to give it a Russian franking and counterfeit frankings from other countries if they helped. This was the tourist season. Thousands of foreigners came and went every week. Customs officials at the airport would be too busy to bother about the wife of a British subject going home with him. Their worst time would be while they waited to emplane.

Her warm hand pressed his flat on the curve of her waist.

'Help me,' she pleaded. 'I will do whatever you want me to do.'

He thought this a bit much. Whoever said that lightning never struck twice in the same place? Maybe he should set up in business as a sort of latter-day Scarlet Pimpernel, a bodyguard for women going into political retreat. A great many risks were involved. It would be far riskier for himself, the information he carried, and for his companions if he refused. He was passionately attached to his neck. He thought through her plan again. Somewhere far back in his mind was a tiny idea which lay like a seed waiting to be planted in the soil of imagination and experience. At present its nature completely escaped him.

'I'll help,' he agreed finally, as if he had a choice. 'But no guns. Promise?'

Irina stopped and pulled him round to her. 'I promise, if you think it best, and will be whatever you want me to be,' she said and laid her open mouth on his.

When they came in sight of the car she was telling him about her father, who had taught English at Leningrad University, and her mother, a botanist, both dead for several years as a result of their war experiences.

He stopped.

Three men stood beside the car.

Her voice faltered to a halt. 'What are they doing?' she asked.

For a moment he doubted his judgment about her. Then he reacted as perhaps he was intended to react. 'Trying to steal your car,' he answered. He felt like a puppet as he started to shout and ran towards the men.

14

At the sound of Silk's voice the three men turned to face him. He had seen pleasanter sights. None matched his notion of happy gracious manhood.

Two might be a twin-set. They were broad and thick, about five feet eight tall and at a guess in the late twenties. Their companion was several inches shorter and a couple of stone heavier and a year or so older. All had wide pale faces with high cheekbones and eye-formations which were the legacy left by the warriors of Chingiz Khan and the later Golden Horde when they ravaged and occupied this area centuries ago. Their open-necked dark blue shirts and ancient drab trousers suggested they were workers without proving it. Both of the younger men had shaven heads as if they suffered from lice. Their companion favoured an old-fashioned hair-style, short back and sides and a neat parting. None displayed guilt. Silk's resolute English dropped dead at their ears.

One skin-head said the Russian equivalent of: 'It's one of those loose-bowelled foreigners and his sow. Let's do him.'

His near twin added: 'We could have a good time with her if we got her warmed up. Sows like her go on all night once they're started.'

Their voices too dropped dead on Silk's ears.

He heard her shoes following him rapidly down the road. 'Stay clear of them,' he called, brave as a hero in a nineteenth-century romantic novel. It was a damn silly warning. If anything happened to him she could not stay clear of them.

As he halted in front of them he demanded: 'What are you doing with this car?'

They looked at him interestedly.

He repeated the question.

All of them subscribed to the theory that actions spoke louder than words. They also believed that mass action would defeat the rugged individualist. They came at him simultaneously. He took two quick steps back to get his balance.

Events swung on a hinge of confusion. A knowledge of the films in his pockets inhibited him with a realization of having to restrict his movements to try to prevent them from being damaged or taken from him. He guessed that if he sprawled on the ground he would have no chance. This trio would obviously feel at home among football thugs. Almost as the thought flickered across his mind one skin-head lunged a solidly shoed foot up at his groin. By luck he managed to wrap his right hand round the man's ankle and yanked it up as his spread left hand collided with the other skin-head's oncoming face and shoved it back on its neck. Both actions were logical, his only bother being to accomplish them together. To his astonishment both were successful. With a yell the man on his right fell full-length on the ground where he grunted pain while his friend gave a moan and staggered back against the car and slid down it like a broken egg.

Silk thought this was marvellous. He had not realized his own strength. For a few moments he had to deal with the heavier man alone. So far that individual had contented himself with being first grinning onlooker and then an emotionally disturbed schoolboy. An expression of incredulity went over his face like dissolving smoke.

Silk did not chance his luck too far. There were considerations arguing against rashness. As he waited the Russian took a tentative shuffle of two steps to the left. It was like watching a baby elephant dance. Silk quarter-turned on his heels to keep all three men in sight. He had nasty half-thought that Irina might attack him from behind but was too busy to bother. Hesitantly the Russian took another lumbering step to his right; pretty soon he should get into a quick-quick-slow routine. Silk took a step back. He had a weird sensation that any onlooker might think they were rehearsing for one of those television time-gorgers which had desperately serious young girls and long-haired youths gyrating to pop music. Out of the corner of his eye he saw the skin-head who had fallen on his back flounder around and collapse on his stomach. No movement came from the other one. Their heavy comrade, solemn, his gaze fastened on Silk as if pinned to him, took another ponderous step to the right. Silk hesitated unsurely. That was an error.

At once the large man lumbered forward across the dividing space with the elegance of an enraged rhino, not an elephant.

There was an interruption.

'Stop or I will shoot,' Irina snapped. In Russian.

Silk almost opened his mouth to tell her not to fire, but remembered just in time not to betray himself.

Essentially her order changed nothing. Having started to run, the heavy man appeared unable to stop himself. He charged forward at increasing speed but changed direction slightly. One of his enormous fists bounced off Silk's chest; it was a wild windmill blow, too unscientific to do damage unless you placed yourself precisely where it had to do maximum harm. Silk was generally unhurt but reeled back across the road as if a force ten gale had caught him unawares, staggering unsurely until he finally lost balance and fell on his back. He saw the big little man rush at Irina. Winded, he scrambled round onto hands and knees, hauled himself off the road and swayed forward to the rescue. Irina was demonstrating her commonsense. She had dropped her bag to free herself, had kicked her assailant on the side of his right ankle and was kicking him again, while he tried to get the gun gripped in the hand she held high above her head. Instead of bending her hand back on its wrist, the stupid oaf assisted her by trying to force open her clenched fingers with one of his hands while his other arm tried to circle her waist.

Actually, Silk did little to improve the situation. His punches on the Russian's head were as effective as a butterfly flapping its wings on a military tank. Maybe the man had no sensitive areas there. His clumsy efforts to get the weapon caused it to jump out of Irina's hand like a cake of wet soap and fly across the road. It fell some eight or nine yards away. Silk did not waste effort. He flung himself full-length on the gun. As he got hold of it a shoe flicked past his head. It had been aimed too hastily to do real harm. He shut his eyes and crawled forward, keeping the gun out of sight beneath him. An expected second and more hurtful kick did not materialize. Instead weak hands urged him to get up.

Unsurely, shaking his head, he dragged himself erect as the car set off down the road. They must have snatched her car-keys from the littered contents of her bag. He saw the solid man still clambering into the back, groping behind him to slam the door as the car gained speed.

Silk lowered the automatic. Irina turned to him with questioning eyes.

'They'll give themselves away through those concealed microphones,' he said. 'Your people will be able to fix the car's position.'

She seemed about to say something. Instead she nodded and crouched down to collect her scattered belongings. He pocketed the automatic and went across to help her. Within a couple of minutes the sound of the car faded away. Neither of them spoke while they collected her things together. He watched her examine each article before she replaced it in her bag. It had been a strange little episode and she accepted its outcome more philosophically than most women would have done.

'Did you lose your other keys?' he asked.

'No. They did not waste time directly you had the gun.'

'Don't worry. We'll be all right.'

'Yes,' she said, and held out a midget torch. Its tiny light flashed on and off. 'I always carry this. We may not get a lift at once.'

'Oh?'

'There are few private cars and hardly any long-distance lorries at present. You take the torch.'

'You keep it. We may meet someone.'

'I am not worried,' she said, and looked at him. 'Please,'

she said diffidently, 'kiss me.'

After a minute she drew away. 'Better now,' she said.

'Yes.'

They got to their feet and started to walk in the direction taken by the vanished car, brushing dust off their clothes as they did so. He kept glancing round at the trees. Those only a short distance from the road were already drowning in thickly swirling shadows. Birches which fringed the road stood out against the darkness, the broken silver of their trunks seeming to have absorbed a measure of daylight which gave them a sort of phosphorescence as night slid over the face of the land. No sound except their own footsteps came to his ears. Even the birds had gone silent, drained of their earlier exuberance. He could feel the late evening heat up against his nostrils, the air heavy with the tangled aromatic scents of summer. He still thought these trees could conceal an army.

A cold hand slid into his for comfort.

Half an hour after they commenced their walk they came to a fork in the road. Everything had gone dark. No starlight put its tawdry glint on the dim acres of mystery overhead. Apart from colonies of bats which squeaked past like vestal virgins searching for sanctuary nothing alive had paid obvious attention to them. Since they started the heat had increased steadily and become more pungent with odours given off from the woods. Irina had used her flashlight repeatedly to prevent their stumbling over the rough surface of the road. Its glow scarcely reached five feet, a weak blur which told them little of their surroundings. She had to use it sparingly to save its battery. Consequently they almost passed the fork when a break in the black mass of trees against the slightly paler darkness of sky on their left attracted her attention. At once she flashed the torch. Her hand stopped them.

'I know this road. It cuts through the trees in two diagonal lines with a straight section between them which runs parallel to the main road.'

She spoke scarcely above a whisper.

He got the idea. 'Where does it come out on the main road?' he asked.

'About three miles nearer the city.'

'A saving.'

'Yes. It may be more. But it's narrower.'

'Rougher?'

'I can't remember.'

'How are your shoes?'

'Their heels won't break off.'

'Let's try it then.'

Her hand gripped his tightly as something heavy blundered through bushes among trees on their right. It seemed to be going away from them. No other sound accompanied its lumpish sort of run. He was pretty sure it wasn't human. In other parts of Russia during harder seasons it might well be a rogue wolf on a nocturnal prowl for food, as foxes still plagued parts of Britain. Gradually the tension went out of her hand.

'A wild dog?' he said.

'I expect so. There are a lot about this year. They are very ferocious. A pack of them was reported to have eaten a baby at a village last spring.'

'Can I rely on you to protect me?' he asked anxiously. 'I'm a stranger here myself.'

She laughed. 'Come on,' she said.

After an interval of silence she said: 'You are a strange man. Gerin was sure you were a capitalist playboy. I told him you were too controlled to let others see your true nature, unless they were friends you trusted. Only fools and men who think deeply can be as casual as you and you are no fool.'

'Several people would disagree with you.'

'Do you ever think about death?'

'I have my weak moments.'

'Does it frighten you?'

'I get more bothered about how long it will take. Delays annoy me.'

After another pause she asked: 'Do you ever think about God?'

'It would be most impolite of me to forget any of my few friends.'

She gave another quiet laugh, almost as if his answer satisfied her.

They were nearly halfway along the straight road linking the two diagonal lanes when they heard a car coming up somewhere behind them. It was travelling slowly, like a tired man going home or a hunter stalking his prey. When he glanced over his shoulder he did not see it but he did catch sight of a pinpoint of light among trees between them and the diagonal road they had left.

'It is those men,' Irina said sharply. 'They have come back to rob us. It often happens. We must hide.'

He spared her his own theories. 'It could be your friends,' he said hopefully. 'Would they have followed us?'

'No. And they are not my friends, only people I work with. It must be those men. Quickly.'

She led them into trees on their left rather than risk any chance of being seen crossing the road. Once again he was shown how thoroughly she had been trained by KGB instructors; she turned instinctively towards the natural place of concealment and kept her fingers over most of the flashlight bulb to screen its glow and directed it downward to prevent it being seen. He saw no possible cause for refusing to accept her lead.

They were about sixty yards up the road and the same distance from it when the car rounded the corner and its headlight shone straight ahead of it.

'Down behind these trees,' he whispered and his free hand rested on her shoulder to urge her down.

She complied without question. They crouched down against a conifer, waiting in the darkness. Whoever drove the car, whatever car it might be, was in no hurry. Once he thought he heard men's voices but it could have been a trick of imagination. To be on the safe side he got the automatic from his pocket. He could sense the amount of tension in Irina. It seemed to come from her like a sort of electricity. Gradually the beam of the headlights came nearer and nearer. As they watched she put a tense hand on his arm. Part of his attention centred on her, waiting for any indication of a sign which would bring the car to a halt and men to where they waited. Without change of pace the car drew level and went straight on. Minutes later he stood up, raising her with him. Her fingers clung to his.

'Shall we go on?' she asked.

'Not yet. If it is those men they'll soon be back.'

Whether it was the same men or not, he appeared to be right. Within ten minutes they heard a car coming from the opposite direction and saw its headlights. They went down again, lying flat on the ground as whoever drove the car veered it from side to side across the road, the beam from its headlights probing among the trees like a searchlight. At one instant the light seemed to scythe directly over their heads. A few moments later the immediate danger seemed to have passed. They listened to the car going away down the road.

He helped her to her feet.

'We'd better get on in case they decide to come back,' he said.

They walked on in a silence which seemed uncanny.

Nearly three-quarters of an hour later they reached an isolated *dacha.* It was some yards back from the road, a small square unpretentious house which light from the risen moon showed to be constructed of plank-board. Behind it and on either side the trees formed three sides of a hollow square. It probably contained only one or two rooms. He put his hand on hers.

'If there's anyone there they may put us up for the night,' he said.

'It may be empty. Or occupied by hooligans.'

'I have the automatic.'

She hesitated. 'Yes,' she agreed at length. 'If it is empty we had better keep our voices down in case other people come to it.'

'You're right. We wouldn't see them. Let's try it.'

She followed him slowly up the overgrown path.

No answer came to his knocks on the door. When he tried the handle he found it locked. At the rear he discovered a window unlatched. He opened it and clambered inside flashing the torch around. There was an old cane chair, a large iron bedstead with a mattress but without sheets or covers, and a small wardrobe. Every wall had almost disappeared below unframed canvases, most of them contemporary landscapes around Moscow plus a few nudes of a dark-haired woman in her thirties whose physical amplitudes made the buxom girl friends of Rubens resemble starved midgets. Everything was tidy and clean. No hint of dust came from surfaces he touched. At his direction Irina climbed in and shut the window. She followed him into the front room.

It contained no surprises. Cheap red and white checked curtains covered the square windows on either side of the door. On the left a cheap kitchen-type table stood against the wall. On the right a smaller table had a large tin box of oil-paints and cleaned hog's-hair brushes alongside sticks of charcoal and rainbow-smeared rags and an empty jar smelling of turps. Elsewhere was a samovar, an ancient oil-stove, an older oil-lamp, two piles of books collapsed onto the floor, and a plaited rush wastepaper-basket. Here the visible wall space between pictures was even less. There were landscapes searching towards an individual style, some very good indeed, some defeated by absence of technique, and others full of observation sensitively communicated. Most of them showed a progressive elimination of the unnecessary. They could be described as decadent because they ignored the stylised mediocrities of Soviet realism. Here was only one nude, a vast canvas by comparison with the others, a huge exultant study of the same woman which rejoiced in and paid sensuous homage to her lavish contours, a fiercely possessive work which shouted the painter's joy in his acreous model. Once again everything was marvellously clean. Silk's fingertips encountered no dust.

He sniffed at the hot flat air. Its aroma of turps was several days old. He decided abruptly.

'We'll stay till dawn. It should be easier to get a lift in daylight.'

She offered no protest.

While he took off his shirt in the back room a nightbird chattered an alarm call among nearby trees. Almost immediately there was a heavy disturbance of undergrowth as some predatory creature charged through it.

He straightened up from draping his shirt over the cane chair. Irina had gone tense. Her silhouette was stiff against the uncurtained window while she waited. Indirect moonlight enabled them to see parts of the room dimly but it would shift away in an hour or so. After some moments she relaxed and merged into the darkness of the wall. Flexing his shoulders, he went to the window and felt a faint trickle of air cool his chest.

'Which side would you like to have?' he asked.

'It does not matter.'

She whispered as if afraid someone might overhear them.

A moment or so later she came and stood slightly behind him looking out over his shoulder at the trees and star-peppered indigo blue wastes above. He turned and saw she still wore her frock. Shadows hid her eyes but he saw a strained non-smile on her lips. Her hand touched his back nervously. She cleared her throat.

'These *dachas* are always airless.'

'It's fortunate we found one empty.'

'You are very adaptable,' she said in a pettish tone. 'Englishmen do not have a reputation for being so adaptable.'

'We still have rugged individualists.'

When she spoke again her voice had dwindled to a whisper. 'Life is strange,' she commented.

'True.'

'I never thought we would be together like this.'

'Nor did I,' he said quietly. 'Won't you feel hot in that dress?'

She gazed at him through the darkness without replying for several seconds and then said: 'Yes.'

As he reached forward to undress her, she shuddered violently. Instantly he stopped. At once her head gave a brief negative shake. Thereafter she waited passively, moving only to help him finish the task. Still silent, she guided his hands to the curve of her waist and let go of them. Her quietness did not last long. Abruptly she came against him, her hands going over his shoulders and back like a token of relief, of welcome, of a fulfilment. A soft breath of words came from her.

'You know I am yours.'

He lifted her onto the bed. His initial doubts proved unjustified. They seemed to share an instinctive comprehension. She clung and twined and enfolded as if they were lovers familiar with each other and reunited after long separation. Without a word she willed him to take her brutally, as if using her body as a catalyst to break his tensions and perhaps her own. Yes, it was possible; she knew, better than other women, the stresses and strain of this life. For a while they were quiet. Then she sought his pleasure with her at a slower tempo. A great wave of emotion seemed to go through her, and he felt her body come alive under his touch. He discovered that she could indulge fierce sensuality with a quality near to gentleness. Yet she remained surprisingly silent for a woman ready to indulge her desires without reserve. At moments when it would be natural for her to give some word or moan she pressed her open mouth hard against his shoulder and her nails dug into his back. And later they slept. On the two occasions when he awoke briefly the night around them was silent.

15

In the sharp early sunlight of what promised to be another cloudless day they walked up the wide tree-lined road leading to Moscow. Most of the thin trickle of commercial vehicles which passed them, the only traffic abroad, was leaving the capital. None of the drivers of in-bound trucks heeded their signals for a lift, droning straight past and trailing thick clouds of exhaust fumes guaranteed to permanently damage every lung which inhaled them. They had seen no sign of any other pedestrians.

Both of them were hungry. A thorough search of the *dacha* had failed to uncover a single crumb. Fortunately they had managed to slake their thirst. On his brief solitary stroll to talk to the trees he had discovered a spring of fresh water at the end of a narrow footpath behind the villa. Alone he had washed, dried himself on his shirt, and taken the opportunity to make sure the films given him by Strelnikov were undamaged; even while half-asleep they had never left his thoughts. Irina was delighted by a chance to wash but had wasted no time.

Since they left the *dacha* getting on for three-quarters of an hour ago a silence had descended on her. His glances at her had noted a frown and saw how her lower lip thrust forward like a schoolgirl worried by some problem. She looked very unlike the woman full of loving and tender entreaty at first light whose ardour and tranquility were enhanced by shared knowledge. This silence had come upon her while they walked. Almost impetuously she had withdrawn her hand from his. A dozen paces farther on she had stepped farther out of reach. Since then she had spoken only to express annoyance at Moscow-bound trucks which droned past without heeding them. Twice she had glanced at her wrist-watch as if worried about the time it might take them to get back if no transport came to their aid.

He broke into her private thunk to ask if she remembered whether there were any *kafes* on the road ahead.

'No, none.'

'Surely it would be a profitable venture.'

'They say Khrushchov had such an idea after he visited America. They are still a long distance apart.'

Her sharp voice indicated she was upset about something.

'I like to think we can tell each other's turn of mind,' he commented.

'No man could know what pleases me better then you do. With you I am myself. I had not realised the act of loving could sweep away every worry.'

'What's worrying you?'

'It is not important.'

'You're lying.'

'I am never awake first thing in the morning.'

'You're lying. Tell me.'

She gazed straight ahead without replying. He let her alone to dwell on whatever had changed her mood. These mercurial fluctuations were unfamiliar to him.

Four heavily-laden lorries coming from Moscow passed them. Each truck spewed its evil cloud of carbon monoxide through the early radiance as it droned thunderously on towards Orel and Kursk. Beside him Irina had straightened up and walked as if she were marching on a parade-ground. Once or twice she kicked savagely at stones in her path. They did the next half-mile at a cracking pace, which proved both of them to be in better condition than he had any right to assume. Then she glanced round as if to ensure they were unseen. Without delay she took his hand and stopped and pulled him round to look at her. She did not conceal the worry on her face.

'I will tell you,' she said harshly. 'I am not coming with you.'

He took the line of least resistance.

'You must, darling,' he said urgently, pleading with her, and took hold of her arms to hold her close. 'You cannot let me go alone now. You have prepared your plans so carefully. How can I possibly go without you? After last night? Don't you want to be with me?' He shook her with rough tenderness. 'You told me you were a primaeval woman, remember? I am equally primitive, a chip off the original Adam from wherever he popped up. You said you were mine. Now you are mine. You will come with me because of that and because I want you.' He shook her more roughly. 'Do you hear? I want you.'

He thought it a pretty good nineteenth-century pre-Pill and pre-property act and pre-enfranchisement speech for eight o'clock on a summer morning on an empty stomach, the sort of chat to have modern schoolkids rolling on the floor in hysterics. It had another effect on Irina. She trembled violently. For a couple of minutes he felt alarmed, afraid she might be genuinely unwell. Almost at once she mastered herself. Gradually her trembling ceased.

She looked at him unsmilingly. 'Please, let me stay here,' she said in a wambly sort of voice.

'How can I? I want you.'

She closed her eyes and smiled unsurely. 'You will be in great danger,' she said unhappily, 'and now because of these hours on top of what I have known about myself in relation to you, as a woman to a man, I do not want you to run the risk. I want to be with you but not at your peril. Do not be afraid. No one knows who you are and I shall never tell them. I swear that on my honour as a Russian. Can you believe such an oath?'

'I believe it because it comes from you.'

'I never have and never will betray you.'

His steady gaze searched her troubled eyes. When he nodded she drew a deep breath and looked on the verge of crying.

'You will come with me.' he told her.

'No, I will find another way to leave,' she said sharply. 'There are several. Through Prague and across the frontier into Austria On a Polish excursion boat. Somehow. I will not endanger your life or your reputation.' She shook her head. 'How can I?' she asked in a thick voice. 'After last night? While I still feel you with me? While I know greater need of you, the reality? What sort of woman would I be to harm the man I love? No, I will tell you now who is your traitor and you can tell your friends.'

'MI yedyem, krasavitsa, mI yedyem,' he insisted forcefully. He tried to increase emotional pressure by becoming the passionate lover, and used the intimate tI, thou, for which there was no true equivalent in the confused Latinisation of Cyrillic into English. *'Moya golubushka, moya syerdyechko, krasota tvoya s uma myenya svyela . . . radi Boga! nye byespokoityes', vam stanyet luchshye zavtra. Pazhalsta, moya krasavitsa, idyom vmeste. Pazhalsta . . .'*

She gazed at him irresolutely. Then she weakened. *'Ladno,'* she agreed, not too confidently. Her eyes were glassy. *'Ya poyedu s vami.'* In a humble sort of tone, she added: *'Spasiba.'*

'Slava Bogu! Pazhalsta, nye byespokoityes'.

'Nyet . . . nyet. Tyebye luchshye znat. Prostitye.'

'Pustyaki! MI yedyem, da?'

'Da,' she agreed unsurely, her eyes full of other thoughts and unshed tears. She forced a smile and kissed him. *'Lyubovnik, pazhalsta, polyubi myenya.'*

'Vsyegda, golubushka, vsyegda.'

'Ya u tyebya pod bashmakom,' she commented wrily, and then, for no apparent reason, added: *'Dorian ochen krasivoye imya.'* Her voice caught and she began to cry, tears spilling from her eyes.

'Vyesyelye!' he told her. He did not know if Dorian was a beautiful name, but, despite her comment, he was more securely under her thumb than she was under his. 'Damn the risks, I want you with me,' he said.

He had no immediate response as he kissed her weak lips. Suddenly she had lost the control and nerve of earlier hours. He gave her his handkerchief and she wiped her glassy eyes. He glanced back down the road.

'A bright smile,' he said. 'There's another truck coming. It may give us a lift.'

It did.

16

When he reached Sokolniki after leaving Irina the thought of the next four days revived with added torment in his mind.

On his walk to the pavilion he reminded himself that he had known they were bound to be one of his ideas of hell. As he saw Strelnikov walk away he knew his internal clock would keep him edgily conscious of every ponderously ticking second through the vile hours stretching ahead while his nerves tried to nourish themselves on a diet of psychologically masticated fingernails. On his return journey from their meeting he had warned himself repeatedly of an inevitable series of *crises de nerfs* about each of the several elements involved, how to keep the films safe and get them out of the country, whether Irina could be trusted, what would happen about the hapless Zakharov, if he would run into a third person who would recognize him, whether he would get food poisoning or fall foul of the water or have a nasty dream which would set him shouting secrets while he slept, if a mouse would bite him. He had travelled back through those bourgeois stations trying to forestall every possible horrid thought likely to catch him unprepared. Such miseries were part of his job. On top of them was his position here. He was as unsafe as any of the present leaders of the Kremlin. It never suited his admirable temperament to be condemned to remain in one place and contain himself in smiling idleness while every instinct clamoured to get himself and his valuable parcel to safety. Each of those things imposed a strain. Collectively they could seem as if he carried a mountain on his shoulders.

Now . . . beyond any doubt these coming days would be worse. Much worse.

No one had ever mistaken him for an impressable fool where women were concerned. Women were here, there too, everywhere, like bits of architecture. It was too late to protest. You just had to be cautious. For instance, you could admire a charming or gracious exterior, and still be suspicious of what was stacked in the attic. Many a sugary bun had gravel inside it. And by some oversight whatever Power or forces had controlled the evolution of Nature's finest and noblest flowers, men, finished the task without consulting him. By some extraordinary mischance therefore the seeds which produced these magnificent blossoms contained trifling faults and small weaknesses, one of which were women. He had few frailties. Drink was no problem. It was not his business if others chose to smoke. Drug-taking was a fashionable fad of idiots, something they had to do because others did it, like all those grubby-haired popstars who made noises for three or four overpaid years and finished on Skid Row or hanging from a lavatory chain somewhere. However, once in a rare while, if the mass intimacy confessionals which obsessed some were accurate, once in a rare while he did discover a landscape which appealed to him and in which he could enjoy getting lost. It was fortunate he did not have an immediate desire to establish permanent residence: his breed only caused trouble to others if they tried to combine conventionality with an unconventional job. Possessiveness was not one of his weaknesses.

He kicked irritably at a stone in his path. While they were at the hut, it was an *izba* rather than a *dacha*, it had surprised him unpleasantly to find how taut his nerves had become as a result of these last days. It had been a more welcome surprise to discover how quickly his tension unwound directly he and she became plain man and woman. They were attuned, free from uncertainty. What went on in a woman's mind at such times he did not particularly want to know—most probably it took a little holiday if it could—but you didn't need to see *The Forsyte Saga* on the box to know that if the man was normal the woman was the one who ensured they were attuned. He had been lucky. At such times some dotty women behaved like the rich Jew listening to whines from the poor Jew in the tragic Mussorgsky's *Pictures from an*

Exhibition or a bank manager listening to someone trying to raise an overdraft.

He veered off the path to walk among the trees. As he nodded at and gave arthritic smiles to the few other exhibitors taking a constitutional to overcome the effect of whatever inevitable party they had attended last night, he knew he would want her during the days ahead. Quite possibly he would want her badly. For once his type of humour was no insurance.

He strode briskly into a still deserted part of the park. Yes, indeed, another aspect of tension. He could still feel her living stir against him, recall how his hands shaped on her firm flesh and how her hands went over him exactly as if she had thought of him and herself as she told him, quickened by the surging tide of life. He could remember much more, including her total silence. It was strange how her claim to be a primaeval woman was proved in silence. Yes, by some quirk of fate they had an instinctive comprehension of each other in this hazardous relationship. And that was strange because she had still been blackmailing him then to help her escape from the country, a demand enough to ensure a man became frigid if not impotent. Instead, most memorably, they rid each other of strain. That was a pretty low rating for what had actually happened between them. To be honest with himself what they had done to each other was always ill-served by words. Words left out the heat, the immediacy, the constant change of phase, the assault on the senses. Suffice to say she was one of those few women with an ability to use her body like a flame to serve her needs and to kindle or quieten it as mood demanded. Momentarily he lost awareness of his surroundings as the eye in his mind remembered how starlight showed a faint sheen of perspiration on her ribs, below the shadow of one breast, which vanished as she turned on her side to lean across and seek his mouth. In silence.

He paused to admire the effect of sunlight on a glade surrounded by silver birch. Yes, he was going to want her because of the woman she had proved to be at such times. But he would not need her enough to get foolish or blow his top. His breed seldom did; they stopped being boys directly they took on this work. What degree of torture might cause him to break he did not know because until now no one had tried to torture him. But he knew he would never go daft or babble secrets in order to get one particular woman; that stuff was pure fiction in this age. Unless there was a rush caused by war, men who were weak about women were never appointed agents. Sex weighed on him like a feather.

He turned back towards the exhibition hall thinking of her silence. After they left the *dacha* she had permitted herself a few endearments, but they were awkward and unsure, the time for them already gone. She had spoken more clearly when her hands guided his about her and took his head down to her breasts. Then she had used silence to speak clearly.

As he entered the pavilion he smiled at a greyhaired couple near a grim-faced Leprechaun.

They were too busy for his colleagues to indulge more than a predictable raillery over his non-appearance at breakfast.

During a lull in mid-afternoon, while Martha Conroy was away having tea, Keene commented thoughtfully: 'From seeing him you wouldn't think he'd have such an effect on them, would you, old son? Hidden charms perhaps?'

Hennessy paced around Silk humming doubtfully, like an art critic peering at a slab of inferior sculpture. 'Some of 'em will put up with anything,' he said philosophically, 'though I'd've thought she might be more choosey.'

'He may use something.'

'An aphrodisiac after-shave lotion?'

'Could be. And now poor Martha's saying she'll take the veil because of him. Poor stricken woman. What a cad!'

Silk shook his head. 'You boys will have to do better,' he told them genially, and felt distinctly unreal. This excruciating bonhomie did things to his stomach. He had once eavesdropped on it at one of those weird two-day company conventions where everyone wears a name-and-place label and oozes endless gaiety as if it were symptomatic of incontinence. 'Jealousy is a terrible weakness,' he warned. 'Try to enjoy what little you've got.'

'What happened?' Keene asked. 'I mean, how do you explain it?'

'We got held up at an art show,' Silk said. 'Private, of course.'

He went to greet a party of Mongolian officials.

After the Mongolians went he was spared another bout of humour by the return of Martha Conroy, who had remembered they were to visit the Bolshoi ballet in the evening and was full of excitement for this special gala performance.

As it was, Martha almost ruined the first part of the evening. She prevented him from deciding how best to prevent betraying himself and concentrate on the thought which germinated far down in his mind while he was with Irina.

Like other teams at the exhibition, they were guests of a sub-division of the Committee for External Cultural Relations. Their box near the prompt corner of the stage in the second tier of the vast red and gold auditorium gave them a fine view of the stage. Light from the vast chandelier and nests of electric candelabras showed the audience was clad in business suits and coloured frocks. You could tell from the clothes that people in the first two tiers of boxes were mainly foreigners attended by Soviet officials while those higher up and in the stalls were Russians.

Silk always thought the ballet should be paid the compliment of silence. Keene and Hennessy shared his view. Martha, imposing in a clinging knitted purple dress and a face-powder which smelled like sweet dust, thought otherwise. Directly they took their seats she became as whispery as a wheat-field in a gale. She continued to whisper as the lights dimmed, the baton plunged, and the rag went up on a revival of the third version of *Spartacus* with music by Khachaturyan and choreography by Grigorovich. Her lament was that she would have preferred to see *Swan Lake*.

As the ballet progressed, Silk felt a strong inclination to laugh. He knew the available fragments about Spartacus, reputedly a Thracian of the century of Christ's birth who served in a Roman legion. Roman historians of a later period claimed that Spartacus had deserted the army, only to be recaptured and sold as a slave to become a gladiator. According to the fragments, Spartacus had disliked the notion of being a meal for the lions in an afternoon of hilarious Roman fun. They told how he led a mass escape of other unwilling athletes who rushed for safety to a perch on Mount Vesuvius. There he established a sort of Mao Tse-tung encampment except that he actually led his reported ninety thousand men against consuls sent to break his control of southern Italy. After several campaigns, and weakened by the usual internal-fraternal wrangles over policy, Spartacus was said to have died valiantly in a pitched battle during a retreat. That was the story.

Later historians doubted if Spartacus had existed. They pointed out that early Roman historians were not renowned for reliability. Some believed he might have been a minor rebel dolled up by Roman writers as a super-Drimachus, a sixth century B.C. Greek slave who also led other slaves in rebellion, who also hopped up a mountain for safety, who also defeated every army sent against him, and who ended with a twist on the St. John the Baptist story by giving his chums his own voluntarily chopped off head so they could collect the reward offered for it. Quite a number of reputable historians believed the Spartacus story arose from an opinion of early Roman historians that anything the Greeks could do they could do better.

From the outset, the ballet was a colossal piece of impudence. Whoever dreamed it up had conceived Spartacus as a sort of idealized adult Young Pioneer, the Russian Boy Scout, and wonderous pure. He dripped courage by the gallon and nearly split his seams with nobility. His panache and rippling muscles had a predictable effect on a bint named Phrygia. Sick with love, she leapt around a boulder-strewn mountainside in a handkerchief-sized gauze slip, presumably to prove herself the loyal and fearless mate of Spartacus. Silk thought the unfrigid Phrygia so alarmingly athletic that any word of her coming round the mountain would surely send a dedicated revolutionary scrambling higher up it to save his energy. Spartacus had other troubles. One was the Consul Crassus, a personification of state dictatorial cruelty. Crassus led a company of chaps in a gear of natty togas, mini-skirts, tin hats and glinty footwear, guaranteed to raise a cheer among trend-setters in Carnaby Street. He too had a lithe wench available for frolics when stuck in a draughty tent up a mountain on a cold night. She was Aegina, a red-wig who wafted about in pale blue butter-muslin and a mood of purple evil. When partly stripped and eager to create an impression she loved being borne shoulder-high on a litter carried by her friend's soldiers. Naturally she got after Spartacus. His response owed more to cowardice than to correctitude. Sparctacus had never heard of free love or divorce or other liberties which brightened revolutionary ardour. He went off to play footsie with Phrygia.

This codswallop had about as much culture as a blade of grass. It was merely ornate propaganda. True, it was madly virile, full of Auntie Kremlin's ideas of what constituted the black and white truths which Auntie would change tomorrow if it suited her. Spartacus and his exuberant bint were like thin shiny white cardboard as they danced relentlessly towards his hero death. It was marvellous publicity for Mao Tse-tung.

During the interval before the final act there was an interruption. Briefly the orchestra was silent. So was Martha. Silk looked round at the quietly chatting audience. Out of the corner of his eye he saw a young man push to the front of a box on the fourth tier opposite. Simultaneously a girl appeared in a box on the third tier at the back of the theatre. From their hands leaflets fluttered down like pigeons landing lazily on a public square. People stopped talking. Their heads turned up and went from side to side. A young male voice was shouting in French.

'Long live liberty! Long live equality! Long live freedom!'

At the back of the theatre the girl's shrill voice was calling in English.

'Remember Jan Palach! Remember Jan Palach!'

Without warning a Czechoslovak flag fell in front of Silk and his companions. It must have come from a box above their heads. It fell slowly, twining slightly and straightening out. It fell on four people in the stalls.

'Remember Jan Palach! Remember Alexander Dubcek! Remember Jan Palach!'

Overhead another male voice was shouting in German.

'Frei Tschechoslowakei! Sieg heil! Sieg heil! Sieg heil!'

This was a genuine event, not a student happening.

Silk found it hard to keep pace with events. All over the theatre people were talking. What Russians who did not speak foreign languages might fail to understand from the voices was made clear by the fallen flag. Behind the man and the girl glows of light told of opened doors as people hurried forward. They were ushers, burly men and women who seized the demonstrators but failed to prevent another shower of leaflets. Two women on whom the flag had fallen were led weeping from the auditorium. Shouts from the male demonstrators became ragged and then ceased. Silk saw five ushers drag the man from the box. Clear calls came from the girl as she battled with two women and a man, then she began to scream. People either turned to see her or were diplomatically deaf. Many jumped to their feet as she wrenched herself free and ran forward with the obvious intention of jumping into the stalls. She was only just saved from killing or maiming herself. Other ushers shoved between the rows of stall seats, raging at people to leave the leaflets alone. Their instructions were not wholly effective. Screaming, the girl was carried out. Belatedly the orchestra started to play.

Silk had never seen a more courageous demonstration. It had needed more than the childish bravado of a normal London Sunday afternoon fracas of students urged on by professional agitators who used them as pawns against an unarmed and indulgent police force. This had needed genuine courage, real guts. Those three were young Davids in the bear's lair. After fifty years of the bear organising Trojan Horse demos to further the aims of Russian imperialism. He had seen clearly if briefly the true face of courage.

He glanced at his companions. Their faces told him nothing.

Not surprisingly the finale of Spartacus was very flat beer. He died under Roman spears, an event evidently intended to give him a Christlike image, with women lamenting over the pierced body and a hint of working-class immortality, a macabre finale for such a piece of nonsense in an officially non-religious state. While it was in progress people were already leaving the theatre. On stage the dancers had become lifeless automatons.

'I shall never forget it,' Martha said when they reached their hotel. Her voice was without its usual affectations. 'Never.'

Hennessy grunted. 'How about a drink?' he asked savagely.

'Better we don't mention it,' Keene said. 'You agree, Foot?'

'Yes,' Silk agreed. 'They may suspect others of being involved.'

He spent a largely sleepless night. At times he thought

of Irina.

Nobody mentioned the event to them next day, the last day of the exhibition.

All Moscow had heard about it. That was certain. But Russians had years of practice at keeping their thoughts to themselves and officials were their normal smiling happy contented selves. Silk contrived to see both *Pravda* and *Izvestia.* Neither paper mentioned it. They were awaiting the Party line.

At the exhibition everyone was busy until the doors closed and the last visitors had gone. Immediately the team of skilled workmen which had arrived from Britain during the morning started to dismantle and crate up the exhibits. With one exception it was the same team which, under Keene's guidance, had done the assembly work and then returned to Britain. They tackled their work with the skill of long experience.

During a quiet early dinner with the others, Silk wondered if he would see or hear from Irina. Since they parted his theory about her had hardened; there was too much evidence for him to be wholly wrong. But she might not betray him.

Alone in his room later he had sharp hurtful memories of their hours together. He would have liked to go for a walk. But this was not a town where a visitor could wander around late at night without attracting suspicion. So he had to let memory take his course. Later he started to wonder about what was happening to the young demonstrators. He doubted if they were having a comfortable time.

At crack of dawn he was up for breakfast with the others and went to Sheremetyevo to see them emplane.

Keene and Hennessy were cheerful at the prospect of being back in London within a few hours. Martha Conroy looked weepy. She stared round the long waiting hall, a cavern echoing with footsteps and voices.

'I hope we come back,' she said. 'I would like to see more of Moscow.'

'Once is always enough for me,' Keene commented.

As they parted Martha said: 'Take care of yourself, Mr. Foot.'

'He'll be fine,' Hennessy told her. 'He has a friend here.'

Silk watched the large Trident gather speed down the runway until its nose lifted and it soared up into the cloudless pale sunlit sky. For a moment he lingered, listening to the sky and glancing around him. Then he went to the ground floor *kafe* and gave himself a cup of tea.'

He sat at a table and sipped it thoughtfully. Now it would be risky. One word from Irina now, one even earlier, and a new untunely voice would be added to angel or other choirs. Somehow though he did not expect her to betray him. Most likely he would never see her again. But he was relieved to be alone; he loathed being encumbered with those classified as civilians. He glanced at an adjacent table where Leprechaun sat pretending to be absent; it felt almost like a tiff in marriage. He finished his tea and wondered what had happened to the demonstrators.

On his return journey he sent Priest a cable announcing that the exhibition had produced some results and he would follow the others home the following day with a good late order.

He spent most of the day at the exhibition supervising the removal of the exhibits and checking lists of Russian governmental agencies which had shown most interest.

By evening everyone was talking openly about the incident at the Bolshoi. An account of it had been given over the radio, forced from the authorities by foreign reporters who had informed their newspapers and agencies. He listened in to Russians discussing it when he took a trip along Moscow River on one of the hydrofoil 'trams.' Their very guardedness gave proof of their feelings.

He went to bed without having seen or heard from Irina. For some moments he endured those recollections which make some men bloody fools over the most unlikely women. As he was going to sleep he realised that any possible trouble would probably come when he went to emplane.

Early next morning before going for breakfast he packed everything ready for his departure to catch the late afternoon airplane from Sheremetyevo.

Fortunately his nerves were calmer than he had expected. Normally when he had a mission in a city they were tighter than harp strings at this point. Additional proof came when he entered the restaurant and was shown to a small window table overlooking the street. He had no inclination to glance round for reassurance; a sure sign. Undoubtedly his tension would increase later, he warned himself. That was inescapable; unlike his departed companions he would not be safe on the airplane because he was booked on a Ilyushin-62 with a Russian crew and inevitably some Russian passengers. And he had no gun which might have given him a slight chance of dominating events for a short while. Meanwhile, praise be, he was calmer than he had any right to expect. There was nothing like a woman to either calm you down or drive you up the wall.

When he left the hotel there had been no word from Irina.

He took the Metro out to Sokolniki.

Halfway through the morning he had what might be the first attack of panic. He had nothing to occupy his mind. He had left everything in the capable hands of Brown, foreman of the team dismantling the exhibits, a grey-haired man with considerable pride in his work and his team. As his nerves started to crawl he took himself off for tea at one of the glass-walled rotundalike *kafes*. Even while he looked at people he dripped with anxiety and felt a slight nausea imagining all the things which could go wrong. Then, as suddenly as it began, the attack ended. When he left the *kafe* he was his own man again.

He enjoyed the walk back through the warm leaf-patterned sunlight to the pavilion.

No one had inquired for him during his absence.

He looked at his hands and saw they were sweating again.

He busied himself with a last glance round at what was being done. At one instant he felt almost like pulling a temperament on the unfortunate workmen just to get rid of his unease. That was out. He had absolutely no justification. Everything was being stripped, crated, and cleaned, with admirable efficiency. Sacking and straw were strewn across some aisles. Voices and hammers vied for domination, echoing dully round the emptying hall. He kept in character by asking Brown about arrangements for transporting the exhibits to Leningrad to be loaded on a British ship which would return to London. Their discussion of details was interrupted.

'Darling, I thought I'd better collect you,' said an English-accented female voice. 'Time is getting on.'

Something cold twisted in his stomach. 'You fret too much,' he said.

She looked at him with eyes full of candid love and knowledge and good humour. He detected no trace of tension in her. Her lightweight woollen coat and skirt of silver grey with thin vertical stripes was undoubtedly of Yorkshire manufacture. Under it the wide soft collar of a dark green silk blouse left her neck bare. Her nylon and pale grey court shoes were of British make. She had changed her appearance. A dark green pill-box hat tilted back on shining brown hair. She used a paler make-up and natural lipstick. He saw the shape of her eyebrows had been altered. Both the broad gold wedding-ring and diamond engagement ring were new to him. Everything about her told of a woman confident of herself in every role. Now he was convinced part of his theory must be correct.

He saw Brown studying her with unfeigned admiration. 'Mr. Brown and I are just settling a few points,' he said absently. 'Then I'll buy you lunch.'

'Oh dear,' she said uncontritely. 'You're in your "don't fuss me, woman" mood.' She smiled. 'We women can be tactless, Mr. Brown.'

Brown rose to it. 'I'm sure you're never tactless, Mrs. Foot,' he said.

She turned aside to let them finish their discussion.

As they walked to where she had left the car she said: 'You look beautiful, like a Greek god.'

'Yes.'

'Were you always so handsome?'

'Mmmm . . . to the best of my memory, yes.'

'I haven't known how to stay away. Your body has haunted me. Have you missed me?'

'You really are lucky to have me. Yes, I've missed you. Where shall we eat?'

Her hand twined in his. 'You choose,' she said, and: 'Those trees over there are close together. No one would see us if you want to kiss me.'

He accepted her suggestion. She fitted herself against him like a sigh and her lips clung to his with something like relief. At length she drew away, smiling up into his eyes.

'I feel better and worse. How are we going to wait until we are safe in London? I shall keep you in bed for a week.'

'Who'll take in the milk?'

While they were having lunch she started to tremble. 'I can't do it,' she said sharply. 'It will be dangerous for you, it will ruin you.'

'We're going together as we decided.'

17

They reached Sheremetyevo without incident.

Nobody paid them much attention as they went through customs. Shermetyevo did not yet rank as one of the world's busiest airports but to him it seemed inordinately full. There were scores of people in the transit hall. Overwhelmingly they were foreigners with a sprinkle of waxy pale Russian faces, guides and spies, and young Russians come to see an airport.

Near the steps leading up to the London airplane was a group of elderly Soviet nabobs in grey suits and ancient felt hats. They were seeing off equally elderly but hatless men, each of whom clutched a little bouquet of flowers. Silk had an idea they were dear old pals from the Comintern and United Front days when Coms dominated socialist party rallies, an earlier decade of Sunday marches everywhere except in Russia. That was also the time when Trotsky and other once well-kissed comrades were bumped off. Over them all hung the shadow of Sergei Nechayev.

'How did you manage to get a seat on this flight?' he asked as they walked towards men embracing like deathless lovers.

'You told me which flight you were on. I told them you had forgotten to check on a seat for me. They had several vacancies.'

Unheeded they passed the leavetakers and climbed the steps. They had no time for a final glance at this corner of Paradise. Game to the end, the old revolutionaries came charging up the steps, cheerful as wrinkled film stars remembered by somebody, flushed with fame past and vodka present.

A pleasant stewardess showed Mr. and Mrs. Foot to seats up front. He felt more than unreal, sort of drunk and uneasy, full of foreboding. If anyone had bothered to take his pulse they would have found it thundering away like a low-level runner trying to sprint in Mexico City. But eventually, without warning, the airplane move forward and turned onto the runway. Within minutes they were airborne. He saw her smooth the palms of her hands down her skirt, a female method of getting rid of perspiration. Nor was she alone; he was sticky most places. Directly they undid their seat-belts the stewardess came back to ask what they would like. There was a wifely touch about the way Mrs. Foot took charge.

'Neither my husband nor I ever eat or drink on a flight,' she told the stewardess pleasantly, and thereby got rid of one of his risks of being poisoned. Except that his original idea had hardened into a conviction which ruled out much chance of poison.

Less than twenty minutes later she was asleep, her head on his shoulder. Behind them the venerable revolutionaries were getting higher on drinks. Their conversation was dated. They discussed varieties of vodka, recalled the women Moscow lent them when they first visited it as energetic young revolutionaries forty years ago, talked about La Pasionara, Dolores Ibarruri, of Spanish Civil War days, as if she were the Biblical Ruth, and Kim Philby as if he had just climbed down from a Cross. Most of them were widowers, he gathered, but apart from recording the death of their wives they never mentioned them, only the grandchildren they were trying to train as good revolutionaries to follow in their footsteps. To a man they were against the needless bloodshed of war. So was he. They were all agreed the revolution was coming, heads would roll, the gutters run with blood. Including, presumably, the blood of their grandchildren. It was all pretty weird and mentally retarded.

He turned his thoughts to more profitable matters.

Clouds drifted over London like majestic swans when the airplane touched down at Heathrow in mid-evening.

Once again they went through customs without incident. He did not relax. After what had happened to the Petrovs in mid-air over Australia and those other Russians at the Dutch airfield a few years later a rush of Soviet Embassy officials to try to drag her away could not be ruled out as a possibility. It only partly reassured him to see a positive regiment of friends watching him and his companion through every stage of arrival. They were necessary. Heathrow was full of people of every nationality about to disperse to every city in the world. There was also the possibility of Arab bombs blowing. Without that chance, amid this noise and crowd one or two people could easily be killed in this lunatic age. He saw Priest and another official face at one section of seats. To his intense surprise, nearby were the three whom he had seen off yesterday morning, all of them wearing very different expressions and as surprised as himself to see him escorting a woman. He was infuriated. Near to blowing his top, he led her to the usual exit. Outside the pavement supported enough plain-clothes men to hold a policemen's ball. One of a group of chauffeurs came towards, adjusting his peaked cap and flicking his jacket with careful fingers. He had never seen this man before.

'Evening, Mr. Foot, evening, madam. Good trip, sir?'

'Not too bad, Charley. Only thirtysix minutes late. How is Gwen's back?'

'Better in this dry weather, sir. The car's up here. Where to, sir?'

Silk had the suffocated feeling of a man unlikely to go anywhere. In one guise or another plainclothes men surrounded him like a thick winter vest.

'Is there any food in the flat, Charley?'

'Gwen thought you might prefer to have something in, sir. She got a steak and ah chips and ah mushrooms, fruit ah salad, and she's done the coffee. Or would madam prefer to go to a restaurant?'

'I would prefer the steak,' she said without hesitation.

'Mr. Foot's a fine cook, madam,' the stranger said complacently, as if he and Silk had been schoolboy chums. 'It'll be nice to relax after your journey.'

Throughout the drive they were carefully guarded fore

and aft by anonymous Special Branch vehicles. Silk felt quite precious. She sat silent looking at the sandwiched traffic. At no time did she appear aware of their heavy guard but she must have known it was there.

He shut the outer door and went back into the living-room where she was wandering round looking at pictures on the walls. While she stood still he eased off her hat and helped her out of her coat and took them into the main bedroom. When he got back he noted that her face showed no sign of fatigue.

'What sort of drink?' he asked.

'Have you gin and lots of ice?'

'Coming.'

While he prepared the drinks she said: 'You want to search my cases.'

'We have things to discuss,' he agreed, and his foot pressed down a ridge of carpet. He took the drinks over and motioned her to the settee. 'It can wait if you feel too tired.'

She nodded meaninglessly and sat down and opened her bag and took out a ring of keys and laid them down beside her. 'Here are all my keys,' she said matter-of-factly as she took the drink from him. 'I will open everything to prove it will not blow up. You must tell your friends I am with you.'

He sat down beside her. 'Give me English gin every time,' he said after he had sampled his drink. 'Isn't it pleasant to relax?'

'You have earned it.'

'Thank you. Actually, they know.'

'Those men I saw.'

'Yes. They don't know you are Irina Gerina, the widow of Pavel Gerin, but they know you have come with information.'

'Will they come here tonight?'

'It depends on how you feel. They will know we are old acquaintances, I shall tell them, and you may prefer to talk to me first. But if you'd rather have them here I'll tell them.'

'Can I talk to you? You give me confidence. I will tell the truth.'

'It's always helpful. Actually, none of these chaps is frightening. You could talk to them just as frankly. You can have one of our girls if you'd sooner talk to a woman.'

'I prefer to talk to you.'

'Fine. No rush. Drink up and we'll have another.'

She frowned slightly and finished her drink at a gulp. 'People in Moscow will soon discover I have gone,' she said as she handed him the glass. 'Will your country give me political asylum?'

He got up and went over to the cocktail cabinet. 'Same as before?' he queried.

'Please.'

'Unfortunately I am not one of those who decides such things.'

'Do you think they will let me stay here?'

'I hope they will. Much of it depends on you.'

'Are political refugees kept under house arrest?'

'They need to know where PRs are while their cases are being decided. People at the Russian Embassy go into their usual waltz directly they hear someone has come out under the wire.'

Her gaze searched his eyes as he went back. She appeared unsure of herself, lonely too. Such moments were inevitable. Usually they were more noticeable among men. Women were great adapters. He shook his head.

'Take your time. When would you like to eat?'

'Can I have a bath first? My skin feels like wet cotton-wool.'

'Of course. Will you open your cases first?'

While she was in the bathroom he undressed and put on his dressing-gown and slippers. She reappeared, padding barefoot into the room as he finished another examination of her cases. He thought she was beautiful with his threadbare old blue silk gown hung loose on her shoulders and her skin still flushed and smooth, wet ends of the strangely brown hair sticking to her neck. As they looked at each other he changed his mind about speaking. Words would have been crutches. Their eyes did far better. Although their mutual tensions were still high, inevitably, there was more than tension between them. More than memory and relief showed in her eyes. And in his own. He wanted her. She recognized it and came across to him so swiftly that the gown slid off her shoulders.

They finished their steaks just before midnight. She had let him cook, exclaiming surprise at his competence. To his relief everything reached its intended end at the same time. No matter what anyone said if you had a butcher who knew how long to hang beef there was nothing to beat a British steak anywhere in the world. When they finished he prepared coffee and found a bottle of Van der Hum for liqueurs.

As he sat down beside her on the settee she settled herself more comfortably with her legs across his thighs. A frown creased her forehead. She looked up at the ceiling as if searching it for words.

'Dorian,' she said at length.

'Mmmm?'

'What do we, what do I, do now?' she asked, and had reverted to her own language. Her thoughts went off at a tangent. 'You British are very strange. No KGB official who had your knowledge of the Middle East would ever be allowed to run such risks in enemy country merely to contact someone who had information about the battle of our intelligents.' After a pause she went on. 'You probably realized I brought microfilms of everything Professor Konuzin intended to give you. There are also microfilms of three anti-Kremlinist novels and an underground play. They are under the lining of my suitcases. On the left side of the small case, also on microfilm, is proof that Jeremy is a man named Julian Monkman. I can tell you the names of two people to whom your government gave political asylum who are KGB agents, buried here for the next four years with instructions to do nothing until your police are no longer interested in them. There are also wreckers at work in America, trying to ensure she becomes soft and that the Army and Navy lose face. I have names of agents at work in your factories and docks and in the Irish Republican Army.'

'You brought a lot of material.'

'Yes,' she agreed, and then looked at him worriedly. 'What am I to do, darling? I cannot stay here. It would be dangerous for both of us. I will not let you be in danger because of me. I am afraid of being kidnapped. I must go somewhere. But always I shall want you to come and see me if you want to. Neither of us is the sort to be married. I must work to get money. I have very little. You understand I am not selling what I brought out of Russia. I am giving it to show there are Russians who try to preserve the honour of their country.'

As she talked she had drunk her coffee and liqueur. Each sentence had come slowly, often broken by long pauses as if uncertain of either the right word or what she wanted to say. She had come up to kiss his mouth and turned to lie on her front.

He let some minutes go as if he was giving the matter considerable attention.

'It's a bit early to start making final plans,' he said at length. 'You don't have to worry about money now. That's the least important thing. And I will find somewhere safe for you to go until you get adjusted. You'll need time.'

She seemed to remember something. 'I am sorry about the trick I played on you,' she said.

'Forget it.'

'No, it was wrong of me to blackmail you.'

'I was a bit surprised by everything happening at once. That was because we were in a city.'

'You also hate them.' she asked as if with relief. 'I too . . . but I would not have betrayed you. I was desperate to come out. Somehow—is that your word?—somehow I have always lacked the courage to come out by myself. Women do lack courage to act in such things unless they are unusual women or have the oldest cause known to my sex. But I would have come. Somehow. You were my chance. Forgive me. . . . I did not want to risk being sent to an asylym and given drugs until my mind was destroyed.'

'I'm glad to have been there at the right time.'

'What can I do?'

'Have you any idea of what you want to do?'

She frowned thoughtfully. 'I would like to write a book about Russia's empire. Why do none of those who protest against imperialism ever write about the Kremlin's empire? Lenin said Czarist imperialist policies made our Russia "the prison of the nationalities". Do you remember?'

'Vaguely. So you want to write about it?'

She nodded.

'Somebody must. It is a bigger prison now.'

He nodded.

She ticked them off on her fingers. 'Latvia and Lithuania,' she said. 'Estonia. Part of Poland. Now Czechoslovakia. Is Bulgaria really free? Or Hungary? Or Poland? Or East Germany? There is pressure on Finland. There are the subject imperialist peoples all the way from Azerbaijan to Outer Mongolia and Siberia. It needs a book to expose the Kremlin hypocrisy. I would like to destroy the mystique about Lenin. You know it is said the only people in Russia who believe in him are still waiting for the Revolution.'

'It's a good idea,' he told her. 'It should have a good sale . . . I'm afraid you'll have to cooperate with various other details of a short while first. You have reckoned on that, of course. . .later on, if you wish, I might be able to keep an eye on your progress. I have a book coming on, about the present state of the West. My typewriter's temperature is beginning to rise.'

Her eyes glowed. 'We could be together?' she said.

'It depends on how you feel. Two typewriters can live as cheaply as one. But it depends on how you feel about it.'

'I would like it,' she responded unhesitatingly.

'You could also help me. I need someone to correct my English grammar.'

She laughed. In the last few moments her face had lost its tiredness and she looked much younger, unguarded, confident of herself in her relationship to him and through that to these unfamiliar surroundings. She smiled like a girl.

'I would like it,' she repeated, hesitated, and then, in a rush, went on: 'I have feared losing you if we ever got here. Other people would be strangers. I meant what I have told you about my feelings for you. Perhaps they were born of my realization of how my people are being misled by the new czars, perhaps it was many things I do not understand at present. But I need you. My mind wants you to help me through these days until I am acclimatized.'

'You'll have to cooperate with other men for a bit.'

She sat up. 'Must I cooperate with them tonight?' she asked, and again in a small rush: 'My body needs you now and will go on needing you. I do not want a man because he is a man. It will be good for us to share things apart from the life we know.'

'Yes,' he said. 'I'd like another cup of coffee. You too? Stay here while I get it. You can find late music on the radio.'

While he prepared their coffee a red pilot-light on the electric cooker glowed twice. Priest and the others had overheard the conversation on the concealed microphones; as much as his foot on the stud under the carpet had let them hear. He added a natural delayed action tranquilliser to her cup and carried the tray back into the livingroom.

18

Soon after seven o'clock while Silk was preparing a breakfast tray in the kitchen the red light came on. He put the butter-dish on the tray and switched off the kettle and went into the small pantry and closed the door. When he slid up the cover of the bread container and shifted a brown loaf Priest's voice came to him through the air-grille behind.

'Alone?' it queried, and he detected a distinctly worried note.

'Yes,' he answered curtly. 'You heard our conversation?'

'Yes. We went after him but he had gone.'

'Do you suppose someone told him?'

'No need. He was at the airport to see you arrive. I had not told him you had gone. He must have recognized her. We're covering the usual exits.'

'A fat of use that is.'

'It's worse than you suspect. At his flat we've found evidence he's a fully qualified pilot. Most likely he had his training under another name and after he passed his tests went somewhere else in disguise for people to get to know him under a third name. A quantity of presumable business executives own planes. By now he may be anywhere.'

Priest only told others what they could figure out for themselves when he was worried.

'Did you get the other material?' he was asking.

'I brought back what I was given. You've opened her suitcases?'

'Yes. We found microfilms where she told you she'd hidden them. Anything else about Strelnikov?'

'We talked. You know the other one was arrested? Incidentally, you should have told me those three were our people. It's an additional worry to believe you have to protect civilians.'

'We had our reasons. None of them knew about you. They were waiting in case anything happened to you. I believe Miss Conroy helped you out at the party. She had realized you were the one on the mission.'

'Tell me next time if there is a next time. Are you going anywhere?'

'It depends on what we learn.'

'Listen in for a bit,' Silk said quietly. 'Things are not what they seem. It's too complicated to go into but I've got an idea about my girl.'

'Will it take long?'

'I need some time. How did the election go?'

'The Opposition was elected to government.'

'Really? . . . well well well . . .'

He replaced the loaf and shut the container and left the pantry.

To reassure himself, he went and looked into the bedroom. His companion lay on her front, arms spread wide, the top sheet pushed down to her ankles. They really were gorgeous legs. You would have to be kinky not to enjoy them. Fortunately he was not too impressible; her body and how she used it, those legs, her strong and shapely arms, her mouth, the obsessive wildness which could possess her, provided a formidable female inventory. At this sight Praxiteles would have started to chip marble. He shut the door and went back.

He finished preparing a breakfast of boiled brown-shell eggs, toast, honey, Oxford marmalade, milk which tasted like it, enough coffee to float a yacht, and surveyed his handiwork with pride.

'*Dobroye utro,*' he said as he went in. '*Pora vstavet, lyezysbaka. Zavtrak.*'

'*Zdarovo. Uzas! Kotor'i chas?*'

She spoke sleepily without attempting to stir.

He put the tray on the bedside table and glanced at his watch.

'*Pozdna, byez chyetvrti vasyem.*'

'*Kak byezit vryemya!*'

'*Da,*' he said, and repeated: '*Zavtrak.*' He seated himself on the bed. She opened her eyes experimentally; their lids met difficulty. She smiled.

'Kak tI pozivayetys, moi krasavyets?'

'Chudn'i.'

'Da, zdarovo,' she agreed, and laughed quietly. *'Nash myedovi'i myesyats . . . nyet, moi myedovi'i myesyats. Zdarovo, yeshyo i skal'ko raz! Moi bol'shoi lyubovnik.'* She yawned deeply and finally opened her eyes.

'Stanyet luchshye.'

'Noch i dyen?'

'Day and night,' he promised and beckoned her to sit up. It was a fine sight. She was beautifully fluid and graceful; she held him close, whispering lavish Russian endearments. Then she shivered. *'Kak dela?'* he asked. *'Spat kharasho?'*

'I slept wonderfully. I feel beautiful.'

'No shock. You are.'

'You are much more beautiful. Men are. Women are so utilitarian.'

'Six cheers for some utilities. Have the eggs before they get cold.'

'Food! . . . I would sooner we . . . yes, we will eat. Must I dress now?'

'I'm in a masochistic mood. Stay bare.'

Over a third cup of coffee he said: 'Tell me something.' He paused and then went on: 'It arises from our luck. We were phenomenally lucky. Me in particular. First, only you knew I was in Moscow. Then came poor Zakharov. No one had told him I was there. He recognized us. If he had gone off to tell someone quietly he would still be alive. Instead he tried to arrest me and died accidentally. If he hadn't he would have told a lot of people he saw us together. That would have embarrassed various officials. Right?'

After some hesitation her head dipped, and she said: *'Da.'*

'Right,' he resumed. 'We knew each other. Coincidences happen. Zakharov was proof of that. There were other things. Those three hooligans who stole your car, making us walk back to Moscow, could have beaten me up.'

'I had the gun I brought for you.'

'True,' he agreed. 'But if one of them had tackled you while the other went for me it could have had another end. As it was I fought the three of them and you waved the gun. But they fought very tamely. They were half-hearted about it. I never lost my breath.'

'They came back in the car to look for us.'

'Did they? We didn't see them. It could have been them. They represented a possible menace. But what happened? We found a deserted *dacha* which looked as if it could give us safety and it had a window open. It was deserted, the window was open. But there was no dust. Only us. Alone. Or were we alone? Every wall was covered with pictures. With you there, and no one else, I would have been a complete fool to spend hours taking down pictures to look for bugs in the two rooms. Luckily, no one disturbed us. Luckily, we had a good rest before we walked on next morning. Right?'

This time she said nothing, sitting erect in the bed, her eyes averted, sunlight moulding her body.

'And at the airport yesterday we were lucky again, weren't we?' he resumed. 'Those customs officials hardly looked at our cases or your passport. I've seldom had such phenomenal luck. Usually at least one or two things go wrong, dead wrong. Instead . . .' He spread his hands. '. . . everything lovely, quiet, peaceful. And I was lucky because you were able to persuade Yuri Pekelis to get you invited to a party where the usual KGB people who act as incitements for tired foreign businessmen and politicians were in full force. Among all those people only you could really expose me, only you could actually blackmail me by threats of exposing me unless I did what you wanted. Help you get out. But you liked me too much to endanger me. I surely am dead lucky. There were other things. Yes?'

She sat still for so long he began to think she might have lost her voice. Fortunately the thought proved unfounded.

'They were wrong to imagine you were, are, so weak that a woman can fool you,' she said at length. 'What do you think of me?'

A broad blade of sunlight lay across her thighs like an unsheathed sword.

'I am not sure about you. Is the material you brought the genuine material promised by Professor Konuzin?'

'Yes. An examination will prove it. Your experts are the best in the world. KGB officers fear your experts. They do not know I have Konuzin's material. . .you said there were other things about me. What are they?'

'They lead me to hope you are genuine. You never mentioned Konuzin when we were near a bug or in your car. You told me to search you for a bug. Before we went into the *dacha* you warned me to keep my voice down. While we were there you could have enticed me to talk. Instead you kept silent.'

'I would not have succeeded in persuading you to talk,' she said.

'No. When we were walking back to Moscow next morning you said you would find another method of leaving Russia. You criticized Kremlin policy on Czechoslovakia.'

She raised her head and tilted it back to stare at reflected sunlight patterning the ceiling. She gave his eyes more pleasure than they got from Moore's faceless orificed bints; the contours were those which fascinated Rodin at one stage. After a lengthy silence she looked at him.

'What do you think is the truth?'

He shook his head. 'I can only tell you what I hope is the truth,' he said. 'Like others you became disillusioned with what the Kremlin is doing abroad and is not doing in Russia. But at every stage you've had to protect yourself. As you said, you did not want to be sent to an asylum.'

'Yes, I am a coward.'

'You wanted a chance to escape without attracting

suspicion. I fitted into it. Jeremy told the KGB one of our men would go to see Konuzin. After Konuzin was arrested Jeremy told them our man would not come. But you visited the exhibition and saw me, told them I was Foot and we had met in Berlin. Now the complication. For some reason they wanted you or some other woman to leave Russia to do something. You seized the opportunity to tell them you could persuade me to bring you out to do what they wanted. What is it?'

Restlessly she stood up and started to walk. After several moments she turned to face him. 'It is simple,' she said, and came back across the room and sat down again. 'Jeremy has a woman friend. She was the agent who originally recruited him years ago and has been his mistress ever since. Last summer a KGB agent in America discovered she had sold information about East Germany to Washington. She told them about East German weapons, the size of its air force, the names of Russian spies in Bonn and of an American army sergeant on the KGB payroll.'

His mind ticked on while she hesitated. 'As you know, the Kremlin is terrified of the spectre of China in fifteen years time,' she resumed. 'It wants to appear devoted to peace in order to conclude treaties with America and later Britain and France and West Germany which will operate against China later. It wants defence in depth ready in Europe in case China attacks. No one in the Kremlin really desires peace. Since the death of Lenin the Kremlin has created a vast pantheon of militarist gods whose only work has been to serve the ultimate ends of aggressive Kremlin imperialism. If your politicians and those in Washington believe the Kremlin wants peace they are worse than fools. Do you believe such lies?'

'I hope the Kremlin can be persuaded its policy is erroneous.'

She gave a sharp derisive laugh. 'What the Kremlin wants for the next few years is to pursue its plan of world domination through fomenting conditions for revolutionary takeovers via unofficial strikers and students,' she said. 'They nearly achieved it in France. If they succeed in Britain all Europe will fall. This woman is an obstacle. They want her removed because she damages Kremlin credibility by casting doubt on the sincerity of its claims to be a peacemaker.'

'I see. So you volunteered to try to persuade her to go back. Naturally I know who she is. Two questions. What happens to her if she refuses? Why did you agree to come? A third—who is being held hostage for you in Russia?'

She answered without hesitation. 'I volunteered for the reasons you have just told me,' she said. 'I have two sisters there. They and their husbands will be disgraced but unharmed. If I had left it until the present rulers are replaced by hard-liners next year or the year after—for having acted clumsily over Czechoslovakia, failing to get Russian astronauts first on the moon, failure to improve agricultural and industrial output—they would have been imprisoned. If Marie refuses I have to tell one of the KGB agents in the Russian Embassy here. He will arrange to kidnap her.'

'Their officials know where you are.'

'While you were out of your hotel in Moscow your luggage was searched. None of the addresses were known. I was frightened Jeremy would learn you were in Moscow and tell them.'

'We are not complete fools all the time,' he commented, 'only three-quarter fools part of the time.' While he spoke he felt round his chin and found he needed a shave; something told him he would not get it yet. He stood up and went to the chest-of-drawers and got a freshly laundered vest and shorts, shirt and socks. 'What else?' he asked as he began to dress.

'My feeling for you is genuine,' she assured him. 'I am not a KGB *prostitutka.* We three, you, Pavel, and I were not characters of an oldfashioned literary triangle. You men were in conflict through your beliefs and attitude to life. He was a good modern Russian. He let others think for him. You think for yourself. Neither of you knew how I, the primitive woman, reacted to you. You crystallized the doubts and disbeliefs I had of what Pavel represented and I saw through their lies. I have not deceived you.'

'Good.'

'It is true,' she said, and her voice was nervous. 'You know our saying, a lover is for a month, a husband for a lifetime. I will want you as a lover for longer than a few weeks but men such as you should never marry. An eagle does not fit into a cage for a linnet.'

'Blimey! Ta. And you would grow tired of one man. In this age many women admit they do. I meant anything apart from ourselves.'

'I can tell you the names of agents who will accompany the Red Army Song and Dance Ensemble on their next visit here. And others who always accompany the Bolshoi and Kirov ballet companies abroad. Some have recently been busy in Bournemouth and Torquay.'

He hauled up his shorts. 'Why is she here?' he asked.

'Several attempts to kidnap her have failed. They believe Jeremy may have to protect her because she has a hold over him. He has denied seeing her for many years. My section of the KGB knew he lied about her.'

He zipped up his trousers and put on his shoes. 'Do KGB agents based in Britain know Jeremy's identity?' he asked.

'No. It would be dangerous in case they defect.'

'Have you any lead on where she may be?'

Her reply surprised him. 'Yes,' she said. 'KGB agents kept watch on the place to make sure she did not escape. She lives at 428 Hathaway Court, Knightsbridge, near the Albert Hall, under the name of Mrs. Wilson. Do you know the place?'

'People have to lead me around London now,' he answered, and went quickly to the wardrobe. He got out his shoulder-holster and automatic, and tested the weapon to ensure it was in good working condition.

'What are you doing?' she asked worriedly as he

strapped on the holster.

'I like a brisk walk after breakfast,' he said and started to knot a green tie under his collar.

'I am coming with you.'

'You have to stay here. Friends of mine are here to look after you. They will come in as I leave. They have already taken the films from your suitcases.'

'When?'

'While we were asleep.'

She was silent, frowning as she stared round the room. In the mirror he saw her lips twist in a tight line, then her eyebrows rose like a shrug of resignation and her lips lost their tension. 'Have they heard what we said?' she asked diffidently.

'I kept some parts of our conversation private,' he assured her. 'It was left to my discretion. Otherwise I have been your only bodyguard until now.'

19

After the three plainclothes police cars left behind the new buildings around Finchley Road the landscape reverted to pleasant and dignified blocks of flats, mercifully not sugar-icing white, which had charmed most eyes since they were erected in the last decade of cultural architecture thirty-odd years ago. And round the corner of St. John's Wood Road was a sunlit queue of cricket enthusiasts waiting to get into Lord's; AWOL schoolboys, a sprinkle of miniskirted girls eager for a chance to ask their escorts to explain the finer points of the game, a galaxy of West Indians in shirts brighter than a Hawaiian sunset, and clergymen of every shape and age, no doubt ready to pray for a peaceful match. A double-decker bus idled along like a schoolboy scratching himself.

It was a magnificent English summer day. Everything looked astonishingly placid. There was even a couple of blue butterflies doing a lazy waltz where the road dipped. A girl weighed down by a maxicoat trudged along with the weary stride of those who favoured the garment.

As they rounded the corner into Maida Vale and headed south towards Marble Arch, Silk's thoughts reverted to the main point still perplexing him about his experience in London a few weeks ago. 'They must have had at least two people helping them,' he said, frowning. 'At least. Somebody drove that car while someone else fired at me. Have you ever heard of a group of double agents working together? Much too risky for all of them. They could sell each other to raise funds when their main sources dried up.'

'I think we can rule out anyone else aiding them,' Priest observed.

'Then what?'

'My theory is that another group of KGB agents, probably men who know you from your spell in the Middle East, followed you unknown to Jeremy or his girl friend with orders to kill you.'

'Arabs certainly do hold grudges a long time. They may also assume I'm involved in something now.'

Priest gazed out at traffic and shops flicking past. Then he said: 'Over-lapping does occur. A second KGB group based on the Middle East would have been kept ignorant of Jeremy. I doubt if more than a dozen or so people in Russia knew his identity. Consequently, they may have been after you for something entirely different, even a personal scheme to avenge the death of Gerin. That has its humour.'

'You think so?'

'Nothing the Kremlin or the KGB has ever done has proved them infallible. Their greatest successes have always come from exploiting the weakness or emotional social idealism or cupidity of others. They were never as intelligent as they pretend, except at exploiting others like Pavlov's dogs.'

'So?'

'I think someone gave another group the go-ahead to kill you. That man who tried to kill Marie could have been trying to frame you. He may not have known her identity. We never found him. So it may mean something is brewing out in the Middle East and they want to kill off opposition now. I'll find out if any ME experts have died in strange circumstances recently. You could go and sniff around. You wanted a desert. Now that things have changed I can give you one.'

When they were driving along Sussex Gardens, Silk said: 'A short holiday would be welcome.'

'Visit your favourite Greek island en route.'

'Yes . . . perhaps someone bears me a grudge.'

'These are violent days among local milk bottles.'

They turned left into the Bayswater Road. A short distance farther on a uniformed constable held up traffic to let them cross through Victoria Gate into Hyde Park. They swung down towards the Serpentine bridge. Here it was one of those timeless summer days of green-leafed trees and brighter green grass under a blue sky which always struck a chord of nostalgia if you were lucky and knew such peace in childhood. Only the long-haired youths in grubby jeans and two girls who wore scarlet Dutch caps above waxy pale faces were unfamiliar. Abruptly the radio claimed attention. Priest answered it.

'Yes?'

A city-based MI 5 voice addressed him.

'I'm outside Hathaway Court, sir.'

'Yes?'

'He may be near.'

'You've acted on that.'

'Our cordon is thin but uniformed units are arriving.'

'What did you find?'

'It's complicated, sir.'

'I have some ability to think.' Priest commented drily.

They heard a slight cough. 'A hall porter let our men into Mrs Wilson's flat after they failed to obtain an answer,' said the voice. 'It was empty. As they were leaving the porter claimed to recognize a distinctive woman's handbag which he said did not belong to Mrs Wilson but to a Mrs Mitchell in a flat three floors up. They went there and the porter let them in. They found a dead woman in the main bedroom. We're fairly sure it's the one we want. She was wearing a grey wig. She was fully clothed and had been shot through the heart at close range. She had been dead about ten minutes. We've found no weapon yet. There were three locked suitcases near the main door containing female clothes, documents, and drugs. We think she intended to leave.'

'Background.'

'Stevens, the hall porter, says the suspect arrived home early last evening and went straight up without going to the bar on the ground floor. He and the woman in the wig were known as Mr and Mrs Mitchell. They did not mix with other residents. Stevens believes the woman did not expect him last evening. She went to a cinema and returned about eleven o'clock.'

'Did the porter notice any pattern to their lives?'

'He says they were in the export rag trade, sir. Both were away for longer periods than they spent at the apartment. Sometimes it was empty for weeks. Accounts were settled through Mitchell's bank. They received little mail. He was there more often than her and she sent him cards from European countries.'

'What about Mrs. Wilson?'

'Roughly the same pattern, sir. She was said to be a widow who worked for a woollen company. Her only friend in the Court was Mrs. Mitchell. Sometimes she was there while Mrs. Mitchell was away. She never visited the Mitchell flat at such times. She told Stevens that Mitchell tried to seduce her once when his wife was abroad. But he went down to see her.'

Priest and Silk nodded at each other.

'Did the porter see him this morning?' Priest asked.

'Twice. Porters here are on late one day and early the next. Stevens saw him last evening and this morning when he went out at about seven o'clock and returned fifteen minutes later. He carried nothing either time.'

'He kept his gun mobile in case the flat was burgled or searched,' Silk said.

Priest nodded agreement. 'Did he have a car?' he asked.

'Yes, sir. He usually parked it in a street beyond the Albert Hall. Stevens offered to find a space where other tenants left their cars but Mitchell said it might inconvenience them.'

'More likely he didn't want anyone to know where he parked it.'

'Yes, sir.'

'Disguise,' Silk said.

Priest nodded again and repeated the word as a question.

'Only horn-rimmed glasses, sir. Occasionally he came back from abroad with a moustache or sideburns, once a beard. He shaved them off at once. Mrs. Mitchell said she couldn't bear hairy men.'

'That was when he went on vacation,' Priest said. 'He must have met her elsewhere.'

An idea occurred to Silk, 'He may be partly disguised,' he commented. 'As she was wearing a grey wig he may have one.'

'Stevens said he was a grey-haired gentleman, sir.'

'What about his car?' Priest asked.

'We have four cars hunting for it between here and the Albert Hall, around the Royal College of Science and the Natural History Museum, Brompton Oratory, up the Brompton Road to Harrods, along side-streets between. Is there anything else, sir?'

'No. We'll be with you in a few minutes.'

He was wrong. Another voice rushed at them through the loudspeaker.

'We've spotted him, sir! He was parked in Cornwall Gardens, near the air terminal. He drove off as he saw us approach.'

'Which way? How long ago?'

'North to Kensington Road. Less than five minutes.'

At Priest's instruction the car stopped inside the Alexandra Gate entrance to the park. He used the microphone and gave his present code name.

'This is a message to all units,' he said, and gave instructions to seal off Kensington High Street, Kensington Road, and Knightsbridge down to Hyde Park Corner. He gained quick answers. A policely voice announced that uniformed men would freeze traffic on Kensington Road between Palace Gate and Exhibition Road to search cars and buses.

Silk started to get out of the car.

'Where are you going?' Priest demanded curtly.

'Well, actually, I love to see things for myself,' Silk answered. 'More significantly, if I wanted to leave a particular area quickly after I had cause to believe the police were after me, well, I would ditch any car I had been using and I wouldn't get on a bus in case it was stopped for passengers to be questioned. If my memory is correct there's no Underground station immediately to hand. But there is a park. And if I was a grey-haired man on a summer morning like this . . .'

Priest said: 'Wait,' He spoke a code name urgently. A cool precise male voice announced that its owner had heard the observations. Priest asked for a search of Kensington Gardens, alongside them on the right, and by police cars along roads in Hyde Park, stretching behind them and going left along the whole distance of the Carriage Road and Rotten Row to Park Lane. His framing of an order as if it were a request showed a nice sense of protocol. Then he cut off.

They got out and started to walk.

They strode into mounting chaos. All traffic along this main artery from the villas and terraces of Kensington and the southwest to the West End was being halted. In-bound motorists attempting to pass stationary buses were confronted by uniformed constables who stopped them and asked for proof of identity. Other policemen scrambled onto buses to question male passengers. Barriers were going up to close off subsidiary streets. Pedestrians at bus queues were being questioned.

Silk saw that official interest was gaining a sour response. Unlike Muscovites, Londoners saw no cause to conceal their irritability. Voices were raised in sarcasm or anger. Across the road a couple of men with military moustaches and manners were protesting at two young constables. Four nuns emerged from a new Vauxhall for it to be searched.

'We won't be able to hold this long,' Priest commented grimly. 'We'll soon have the press here.'

'This lot may contain some getting the scene before calling their desks to print it into midday editions.'

They turned right towards Kensington. Its Gardens were on their right, a fine stretch of tree-shaded lawns bisected by paths and drowsy from weeks of phenomenally uninterrupted sunshine. Across the road several cars and taxis had slewed in alongside the Albert Hall to debouch musicians arriving for a concert rehearsal. Their vehicles were being searched by policemen from a Panda.

As they walked on uniformed constables came to question them and went off as men from the two cars which had accompanied them down from north London flashed authority at them.

A police helicopter looking like a hornet clattered into sight above the Albert Hall.

'Strange thing to do,' Silk commented. 'Kill her.'

'She may have tried to blackmail him.'

'Women do the damnedest things but why compound the crime?'

After a pause Priest hissed sharply. 'He could have found out she was a double agent,' he said.

'If he did . . . if he let his owners believe he killed her because she was a double agent, they'd have cause to pay attention rather than discard him for being associated with her. Are you with me? No one in the KGB would help anyone connected with a double agent but if he could persuade them to believe he killed her because he learned she was a double agent, then he would appear like a martyr for the cause. And if we catch him . . .'

' . . . they would have reason to help him escape from gaol if he gets a life sentence which is truly a life sentence. Like George Blake.'

'Yes.'

Priest went off at a tangent. 'I gather an opinion you think your companion may be reliable,' he said.

Silk glanced round from side to side. 'Think and maybe are the operative words,' he agreed. 'It might be a good thing if you let me alone with her. I was promised other items, quite apart from what Konuzin passed to her. Our being here now is one indication that her material is authentic.'

Priest nodded. 'Right,' he agreed. 'Can you give me an idea what those other items are?'

'Roughly,' Silk answered as they neared an old match-seller at the approach to the Albert Memorial. 'Washington will be intrigued.'

He did not add details now. Instead he tripped Priest, telling him to cushion the fall. As they sprawled down two bullets destined for one or both of them whipped above their heads. A man behind them cried out and pitched headlong. Women screamed. Some people fell to the ground for protection. Others stood their ground either from traditional British phlegm or because they were confused by a telescreen incident in real life.

'Don't shoot!' Priest and others were raving. 'We want him alive!'

Silk added his voice. He had no particular wish to spare the Memorial, towards which Jeremy was running; it did not rank among his favourite bits of Victoriana. Even on a day like today it was a pretentious mess in the worst possible taste. But Jeremy was racing towards it, running well for a supposedly old man selling the boxes of matches which had pitched off in every direction as he fired from under the tray slung round his neck. He was a comic figure with a battered old grey hat perched on his untidy Beatle style grey wig and a shiny black maximac which reached his feet and billowed out as he ran. He bounded up the steps to the Memorial flinging off the tray as he did so. When he reached the top he turned and fired at the men racing after him. A plainclothes man stood up on his toes and fell on his back.

Silk scrambled up and helped a briefly winded Priest to his feet. As they joined the rush of uniformed and plain-clothes men they had a clear idea of Jeremy's intention. If he could get beyond the Memorial to the Lancaster Walk pathway he could turn down the Flower Walk or cut across the grass among the trees to one of the other walks which led to exits on the north side. They saw him race like a wild black shadow beside the elaborately carved base of the Monument, its gilt and enamels and various metals glinting in the sunlight, and then he managed to shed the hampering maximac and vanished behind the edifice. They heard two shots in rapid succession.

'If he gets out of here,' Priest said heavily, 'he may pick up a taxi and get to an airfield.'

Beyond the Memorial they found a uniformed constable lying still facing the bottom of the steps. His arms were outstretched and his helmet had rolled off. Some yards away another man was getting to his feet. Everywhere people were running for cover. Nannies had stopped and were calling to children in a variety of foreign accents.

Jeremy ran on and seemed to be drawing away from his pursuers.

Even as Silk thought the man would escape something happened to the running figure. It seemed to jump into the air and almost at once they heard a great cry of pain. Then he fell full-length and rolled over and over, crying out. Silk had seen a similar sight at athletic meetings when runners had pulled a hamstring. Within seconds the fallen figure was out of sight behind a crowd of uniformed and plainclothes men.

When they got back into the car Priest said: 'You'd better spend the rest of the day as I suggested. Or did you suggest it?'

Silk did not answer immediately. He felt most peculiar. Everything had tied up. He couldn't remember it happening before. In espionage there were always the loose ends of a continuing battle. He was positive such neatness must be a flash in the pan. It wouldn't happen again. Miracles never happened twice.

'Would you mind if I have a little celebration this evening?' he asked.

'We'll see how the day goes.'